Subito Press | Boulder, Colorado | 2011

Alta Ifland

Death-in-a-Box

Subito Press is a nonprofit literary publisher based in the Creative Writing Program of the Department of English at the University of Colorado at Boulder. We look for innovative fiction and poetry that at once reflects and informs the contemporary human condition, and we promote new literary voices as well as work from previously published writers. Subito Press encourages and supports work that challenges already-accepted literary modes and devices.

2010 Competition Winners
Fiction: Alta Ifland, *Death-in-a-Box*
Poetry: Andy Frazee, *The Body, The Rooms*

Subito Press
Boulder, Colorado
www.subitopress.org

© 2011 by Alta Ifland

Library of Congress Cataloging in Publication Data available upon request

978-0-9831150-0-7

Generous funding for this publication has been provided by the Creative Writing Program in the Department of English, and the Innovative Seed Grant Program at the University of Colorado at Boulder.

Grateful acknowledgment is made to the following publications in which these stories first appeared: "Death-in-a-Box" in the anthology *Tartts Three* (Swallow's Tale Press), "Double Lives" in *The Redwood Coast Review*, "No One's Story" in *Action Yes*, and "Uncle Otto Plays Chess" in *The Nervous Breakdown*.

Contents

Death-in-a-Box ... 07
The House of Time ... 11
Double Lives ... 14
Going Back ... 17
Shattered Hourglass ... 20
Mrs. Q's Drugstore ... 24
No One's Story ... 26
The Experimenter in Feeling ... 28
The Missing Hand ... 31
Stubborn Memory ... 33
The Girl in the Hat ... 35
The Garbage Woman ... 39
Fried Brains ... 49
Uncle Otto Plays Chess ... 52
Twin Sisters ... 63
False Memories of Not-Myself ... 70
What Would You Do? ... 82
From the Diary of an Accidental Housewife ... 88

Death-in-a-Box

In the days when Death wasn't hidden behind a plastic door in a rectangular-shaped odorless funeral home, but was Life's sister, Beauty was clothed in the enigmatic glow of Death and walked in its shoes; then gradually, Death's mischievous twinkle in the eye was replaced by icy terror. But when I grew up, some people still remembered Death's playfulness and thought that if only they could beat it at its own game, they would eventually cheat Death and escape its inexorability. My godfather was one of them. Of his wife, only a black-and-white marriage photo had been kept, with the groom and bride immortalized in their starched stiffness, and the bride, with that look only Death can put on certain young faces, as if it were the real groom, the bride with that misty Death-suffused gaze drifting toward nothing and already conjuring up nothingness. For this bride's theft my godfather couldn't forgive Death, so he decided to catch it and lock it up in a box.

I should say here that boxes had a particular significance in our family. To begin with, I was—and still am—a passionate box collector. I collect them in all sizes and shapes, from the very small to the big ones, but I usually prefer rectangular wooden boxes. As a child, I kept them in a locked cabinet, each of them inside a bigger one, like Russian dolls. In our house, the long hallway, which crossed it from one end to the other, stopped in front of a storage room full of broken or discarded objects, sculptures missing an arm, bicycle wheels, dolls deprived of their heads, a box of walnuts for the Christmas cakes—which we didn't celebrate, but we did have Christmas cakes each year and called them "December cakes"—various parts of my brother's mutilated toys (soldiers or cars), and, in the middle of it all, a huge wooden box made of cherry: the forbidden box.

"Under no circumstances should you open that box!" my mother told us.

"And if you die, can we open it?"

"If I die and you open the box, you'll be struck dead on the spot."

Dozens of times we opened the door and knelt by the dark box, smelling it and touching it lightly, as if to see if it would open itself to us and let us see its secret. But never, never did we even consider lifting its lid.

And yet, the day came—and how could it have been otherwise—when, after entering the storage room and kneeling by the box in the empty house full of unbearable silence, *I knew I would open it*. And although I didn't entirely believe that I would be struck dead on the spot, I was convinced that my deed wouldn't remain unpunished, not so much by my mother, as by the box itself. *By what was inside the box*. I closed my eyes and tried to regulate my breathing. I thought of all the possibilities. To go on without opening the box. Or ... to open it and then ... I stayed near the box for minutes, attempting to find a little hole through which I could peek and thus cheat both myself and the box. But the wood was perfectly smooth, without a single hole in it. I stayed and hoped for a miracle.

I don't remember how or what I felt when I finally lifted the lid, but I did it. I opened it without looking, at first closing my eyes with all my power, then turning them toward the ceiling and staring at it until I finally found the strength to look inside. I thought my vision was blurred. I blinked several times and looked again. There was no mistake: in the box there was . . . nothing. Absolutely nothing!

What kind of a joke was that? I kicked the box, angry. Then I thought that maybe my brother had taken whatever was inside—but how could I find out without betraying the fact that I looked? I certainly couldn't tell my mother. And as for my father, he didn't exist, or rather, he existed as a shadow that carried a newspaper around. Maybe it was my father who had been hidden inside the box, and then annihilated through some kind of sorcery—it was quite possible, my mother was capable of anything. Maybe we'd been eating his limbs and organs for months, and the box was now empty, waiting for its new occupant.

I blinked again. Or maybe ... maybe someone's Death had been hidden inside the box, and it only needed one little moment to jump out and go into the world to find him. I quickly closed the lid. It was Death-in-a-box. Deathinabox.

Soon afterwards, my godmother died. I can only blame childhood's insouciance for the fact that I didn't even feel guilty. On the contrary, I felt slightly proud for being the only one in possession of this incredible secret: that one can hide someone's Death in a box, and I began to act in accordance with the importance of the secret I held. Thus, one day I entered a Jack-in-the-Box and, instead of asking for a burger, with the most candid eyes and sweet voice, I said, "Sir, could I please have some Death-in-a-box?"

I didn't wait for the poor clerk's reaction; I was out in a second, enjoying the triumph of my courage all by myself.

But apparently I wasn't the only one to know the secret, for one day, while visiting my godfather, I saw him holding *our* box, as he was talking to himself with glassy eyes and transfigured features. The box was open, like a net extending its invisible arms for some fish or at least a butterfly, and my godfather was murmuring with the chanted voice of someone casting a spell or trying to lure an inflexible lover into his bed, "Come here, dear, dear Death, oh come here! Come back in the box! Back-in-the-box!"

Was he hoping to catch back his wife's Death? Whatever he was trying to do, I thought he was very funny and ran out to fetch my cousins; then we all came back and circled him, with pink lollypops in our mouths, screaming and mocking him, as we jumped up and down on the floor. And he kept chanting, "Come here, dear, dear Death, oh come here! Come back in the box! Back-in-the-box!"

We laughed so hard our mouths hurt. We left my godfather there, hopelessly chasing Death, and when I returned in the morning, I found him inside the box, with his limbs stiff and his eyes mirroring Death's petrified gaze. I touched him. And when I felt his coldness, I fled, yelling at the top of my lungs, "Death is back in the box! Back-in-the-box!"

The House of Time

Somewhere, on top of a hill, there is a two-story solitary house made of red brick and surrounded by desolate fields whose skies are crossed only by gray birds on their way south. The house is old, in an austere Prussian style, and its cold, impersonal exterior would never let one guess what hides inside.

The first floor is the baby floor. Dozens of babies in little wooden cribs are zealously exercising their vocal chords and digestive tubes for a lifetime of ceaseless bodily maneuvers. In their desperate cries, a war for power is being subliminally fought, a war in which the one who cries without interruption for the longest time is the winner. Some of them are smeared in their own excrements, others are gleaming with blinding whiteness, as if they have just been changed, and others are crawling on the floor, already flirting with each other or setting invisible barriers for their territory, in which they amass toys for their own pleasure only. But all of them, at one moment or another, are opening their mouths into a screeching scream, unless it is to suck on the breast of one of the nurses who come to feed them every several hours.

The nurses are all dressed in pink. They smell of vanilla and powdered milk, and have soft gestures that seem to muffle for an instant the decibels of the screams. When the nurses enter the large room—one nurse for each baby—they look like a compact battalion without a general; it could be said, however, that each one of them is her own general. Their softness doesn't stop them from being firm and enforcing the rules for each baby with the same unflinching inflexibility.

It is, of course, impossible to say what the babies feel or think when they see this battalion of unsmiling women in pink—the babies themselves are all in white—if they are scared or, on the contrary, happy to see the source of their daily nourishment. But what is certain is that they do take advantage of both the swollen breasts and the milk bottles, and for hours they do nothing else but suck, their blue eyes transfixed by a vision only they can see.

After they are done eating, their diapers are changed, and the nurses spread oils and creams on their tender, reddish skin, and dip them in white powder like chickens in flour. Then the babies go to sleep. For a while. And in the House of Time time stays still, hanging over an abyss of silence, while everyone sleeps.

The second floor is the old men's floor. For each baby on the first floor there is an old man on the second floor. One could almost say that each old man is the incarnated image of one of the babies, ninety years later in time. But of course no one can make such precise statements, and in the House of Time words don't count. Words simply glide on a slide at whose end a black hole awaits to churn and turn them into garbage-like disposable ground matter. For the old men words are like petrified baby screams, screams they would like to be able to let out, but can't. When they open their mouths to form sentences, the words are swallowed by saliva, their mouths dribble, and the nurses need to wipe them like babies.

What do the old men think when the battalion of nurses enters their room, armed with medicine, vitamins, thermometers, and meals soft enough for their toothless mouths? Are they frightened of the nurses' occasional roughness and the pitiless administration of their daily necessities? Or, on the contrary, are they happy to see the only pink light, so to speak, in the morose routine of their lives? The old men, however, are not allowed to suck on the nurses' breasts, but their faces light up and their mouths dribble with excitement whenever the nurses touch them. After they are done eating, the old men's diapers are changed, and whether the nurses massage them with cream and oils or not, the old men are happy. Then, they fall asleep with their mouths open.

Except for the nurses, there is no connection between the first and second floor. Each age has its own floor, but time is ageless and makes no distinction between its servants.

Double Lives

Toward the end of the twentieth-century, humans were so used to transforming everything into something lucrative that they discovered how to make a profit of the last remnant of uselessness: pure being. Until then, they had lived for thousands of years as all other creatures did, content simply to be, with no purpose other than the experience of living itself, joyful or tragic, as the case may have been. But at some point, before the end of the millennium, they realized that living itself could be converted into money or at least into a moment of glory that would justify the otherwise useless existence they had been living, and give it a new, useful meaning. Whatever life bestowed upon them—be it a tragic love story, the death of a child, the loss of a limb or of their eyesight, or even the past long forgotten lives of their ancestors—everything, they realized, could be material for a monument incarnating the experience of life itself, and this material could be offered to millions of souls for consumption, like a magical formula that would tell them how to live. Life stopped being a disinterested passage of time and became the pursuit of the formula's perfect fulfillment.

The new institution that made official the bestowal of meaning upon their empty lives was called "the book contract." It was no accident, of course, that this institution appeared at a historical moment when the book was living its last moments. Humans had known other types of contracts during their long existence as a species, but it was the first time in their history that the contract became the primary term in the equation, while their lives, without which the contract wouldn't have been possible, were secondary. Little by little, they learned how to live according to a contract that was maybe unwritten, but which told them that if they had a certain experience, the official book contract would soon follow, and their experience could be duplicated into something exterior, something they could see from a distance as a reflection of themselves that would be the unquestionable proof that they were alive.

They began to take trips not for the pure sensation of being there but with the idea that a *useful* experience might come out of it, and eventually, a book contract. They went to dangerous places, to wars even, so that they could write books about what they called their "experience." Yet, their experience was merely the prelude to the only thing they were now capable of experiencing, that is, exchanging the image of what they had attempted to live in order to have an "experience" for a book contract. No matter how devastating life's trials might have been for them—wars, tortures, rapes, prison—whether they had been the victim or the butcher, everything was cleansed and transformed into something higher if they signed the book contract. Thus, experiencing horror— the dark face of life itself—became a commodity everyone was chasing because it was one of the last things that hadn't been yet on the market. Poverty was also sought after. The rich were trading days of their lives with the poor so that they could each have the "experience" of the other's life. Everyone was playing a role, afraid that the next-door neighbor might have already acquired the rights to the only unplayed role that was left. Life became a mimicry of itself, a mimicry everyone called "experience."

Yet, what exactly they were experiencing wasn't clear. Was it the dim memory of a time when people still lived without the need to *see* themselves living? Was the "experience" the only proof they now had that they were still part of the kingdom of living creatures? Did they need the contract to prove to themselves and to everyone else that they were alive? That they were not the only species in the history of the planet that was dead, dead but bursting with energy like their multiple-task, marvelously smooth, hollow machines?

Going Back

> "... great men of inaction, among whose
> number I humbly count myself ..."
> FERNANDO PESSOA

Today, as I was tying my shoelaces, it suddenly occurred to me that everything we do in life, every single insignificant gesture points to the future, whether we are conscious of it or not. Take for example, the act of tying your shoelaces: you do not tie them just for the sake of it, you do it because you are *getting ready* to exit your apartment. You are moving toward something that hasn't happened yet and which is part of the future. Or, when you cook, you do not merely act in the moment, chopping onion, and garlic and carrots; you are preparing the content of a scene which will take place in the near future (*le futur proche*), a scene with a steaming dish on a table draped in a white tablecloth, and silverware placed in front of every seat.

So, as I was fastening my laces, I was suddenly struck not only by the orientation of our entire being toward the future, but by its arbitrariness and unfairness. Unfairness to the past, of course. Why shouldn't we do something with the intention of recovering the past? Why shouldn't I, for example, fasten my shoelaces with the *intention* of unfastening them as soon as I finish fastening them, then trace my steps back toward what I was doing prior to fastening them? Now, I realize that if I fasten my shoelaces with the intention of unfastening them, this already points to the future, even though this future is the photographic negative of the present. Maybe I shouldn't tie my shoelaces at all, maybe I should just start by tracing my steps back to what I was doing prior to … to what I was doing before I decided to tie my laces, which in the end I didn't tie. But in this case, there must have been a point in time and space when I stopped, cutting off all possibility of moving towards the future, and decided that I would go back. Does this mean that I can never naturally go toward the past in the same way I go toward the future? This cannot be, I told myself. The problem is that, like everyone else, I have trained my brain to always move towards the future, so therefore I must now untrain it.

This is a day in what I call the program for the defuturization of my brain: I get up and instead of putting my clothes on, I take them off. This means, of course, that when I went to bed I had them on. Then, instead of making my coffee, I first wash the dirty cup, which means that a dirty cup is already waiting for me in the sink—which has always been the case, anyhow. Only after washing the cup do I begin to make the coffee. But then I stop, confounded by an unexpected problem. If I truly want to go toward the past, to move backwards from the present to the past, I must first drink the coffee, then make it. I ponder this new, very serious question. As with the dirty cup, there is only one solution: to have the coffee already waiting for me. Yes, to drink the coffee (which I will have prepared the previous night), then make the coffee (which I will drink next morning). But if I have to prepare in advance my way toward the past, doesn't this defeat my very purpose? Won't I anticipate the future in order to better trace my steps back? Again, I ponder the dilemma and decide that only a servant could help me find a way out. I would have a servant who would prepare everything in advance for me, so I could undo it every morning. But wouldn't this be cheating? Passing the responsibility of the future on to the poor servant so that I can better enjoy my retreat into the past? And, besides, wouldn't this make me part of an endless cycle of doing and undoing, in which more energy is spent in order to go toward the past than it would be to simply go toward the future? Wouldn't this make me a pawn in the field of what I hate most in life—aside from being awake—action? Isn't there any way of resisting the future without *doing* anything?

At this point, I decide that I'll spend the rest of the day rocking in my chair and imagining that I am tying my shoelaces, then untying them, tying them again, untying them ...

Shattered Hourglass

We think we live inside time, but time doesn't exist. What exists is our body holding our mind within it, which thinks of us as time-driven creatures because we see time in the eyes of others. But the eyes of others don't always exist in the same time with us; sheets of parallel times separate pairs of eyes from pairs of eyes like curtains of gray rain interposed between parallel worlds. Does time run in infinite circles, does it fall drop by drop into the mouth of the hourglass or does it spread in long sheets of parallel worlds between which no communication is possible?

A young mother wakes up in the morning. She wraps herself up in the turquoise robe of plush softness that awaits her day after day, then she wraps herself up in the morning coffee aroma, and thus wrapped up, sinks into an armchair, giving herself to oblivion until the arms of her child hold her from behind, their heads touch, then, the child curls up next to her with a picture book and demands—a request uttered with the tiniest voice possible—that she read to him.

Do this woman and her child—this woman of turquoise plush and her child of golden light—exist *in the same time* as the mother and child at whose door a knock is heard in the night, then hoarse voices followed by men in uniform who enter with their heavy boots and take the two—mother and child—to a place of no return? A place where mother and child will be separated, thrown in cells with other anonymous breaths, then ... darkness.

Can the first mother even begin to imagine the anguish of the second? And what if the second—the one now in the dark cell or in the torture chamber—had once been the first woman in the turquoise robe? What happens to time when the first woman becomes the second? What happens to time when the second woman exits the torture chamber? Can she ever return to her incredibly soft chair and her turquoise self? If time flows through us, what becomes of it when a man is on a surgical table to be experimented on? How does he feel time when a doctor operates on him without anesthetic to see what his pain threshold is? Can this knot of pain lying on the table like raw meat have once been the luminous child with golden smile, resting his head on the mother's breast and listening to her voice which he knows from her womb, when time was measured in warmth and flashes of eternity?

Now the doctor is lifting his arm holding a saw, yes, a saw with which he intends to cut off his patient's head. The doctor has eyes, a nose, and a mouth like all of us. He has a brain and sensory centers like all of us. His mother's image floats somewhere in the past, between night and fog. But she was once alive. She was ... Could it be possible? Could the mother of the creature that now holds a saw in his hand have once been the woman in a turquoise robe, a woman who told tales with elves and nymphs to the little boy who would one day cut off someone's head with a saw? Where are the two mothers now? The mother of the one with a saw and the mother of the one to be sawed? If they both live in the minds of their boys, that is, in their bodies, does this mean that one will witness—and even be part of—the savage killing of the other? When playing with her little boy, her child of sun and light, can the first woman imagine that there is a time already waiting for her in the universe of possibilities, when she and her son will be the killers of the second mother and son?

Now the first woman turns on the TV. A bomb has exploded again somewhere. Bodies soaked in blood are transported on stretchers, and faces expressing worry and fear tell again and again how it happened. The woman in the turquoise robe sighs, then changes the channel to something more cheerful.

Meanwhile, the second woman, who also wears a turquoise robe, also turns on the TV. She sees the carnage, sighs, and changes the channel. Lets her body fall into a black leather armchair and starts browsing a glossy magazine while sipping her coffee. The coffee is hot, so she takes her time. But all of a sudden, her arm stops in the middle of its movement, paralyzed. She has just realized that her son was supposed to be on that train. The train with the bomb. Between the two moments—the moment when she takes a sip of coffee and the moment of realization—something has happened to time. But what? Even after the second woman realizes that her son could be among the dismembered bodies, time continues to flow in the same way for the first woman.

Now let us imagine the first woman in front of a computer screen, playing with time. The screen is turquoise, like her robe, so she seems to have descended from the screen itself. In the morning she lives in the Middle Ages; has male friends who go to war—"which one?" you might ask, as if it mattered—and girlfriends with whom she exchanges information about apple pies, curious skin rashes and the various worms she finds in her stool. In the afternoon she is a child, a boy with a golden smile. Could she be her own child? Indeed she could. As a matter of fact, she is. Does her child live in the time of her own childhood, that is, in the past, or does he live in his own time, that is, in the future? Who knows, maybe he lives in the Middle Ages. He lives in the Middle Ages and goes to war. Or maybe he lives in a time of gray metal, and everyone he knows lives in front of a blue screen in which their doubles live in the Middle Ages and go to war and remember the never-ending past? Or maybe her son exists only at night, when she turns off the computer and goes to his empty room and remembers—suddenly remembers!—that he died two months ago in a war which, as the President assures her—on a screen—"goes as planned."

Suddenly, she becomes the second woman. She becomes the second woman and her body lets out a scream that breaks all the screens in the house, and the windows, and, in the end, the hourglass, and time gets out of bounds, and the hours spill out and shatter like glass, and their pieces fly in the air like broken vessels, and her scream covers the city, then the country, and at the end of the night the entire country has drowned in her scream.

Mrs. Q.'s Drugstore

We never go to the market. We always hold each other's hands, dirty with chocolate or caramel fudge, and our hands get stuck, so we have to hop around together, all three of us, like toy bunnies. When we sit down, we need a big surface, so we can all fit. People say we look alike, but in fact, if one looks closer, one can see that we have very different noses and jaw lines. It may be that what people see is not our faces, but our faces *behind* the glass—the semblance of our faces.

We spend most of the time at the window, watching the world outside, the white snowflakes if it's winter, the green pastures if it's summer. We particularly like the flowers with their patches of color like bright paint, and the children, who, one can tell from their open mouths, are laughing and screaming from the top of their lungs.

What we can't see, we imagine. We imagine what lies behind the hills or the other houses' curtains; most of all, we imagine textures and smells. We know the smell of smoke from our own chimney, but we don't know and cannot imagine the smell of roses. We once smelled a daisy, but it didn't smell like anything we knew, except maybe paper. We touched it and it seemed fragile, yet not quite as fragile as we imagined flowers to be.

What we imagine over and over again is the smell in Mrs. Q.'s drugstore. Of course, we've never been in Mrs. Q.'s drugstore. We made a list of the things she must have at the counter—coffee, fudge, tobacco, popcorn, popsicles—and imagined each smell in turn, and then tried to imagine all of them together, but it was hard.

In our dreams each of us enters Mrs. Q.'s drugstore alone, without the other two, and this gives us such exhilarating freedom that we seem to be flying through the store, followed by Mrs. Q.'s severe gaze. She cuts our flight short and asks, "What do you want, kid?"

And then ... we don't know how to answer. We can't remember any of the things we covet from the long list we made, and she chases us out, calling us "shameless little thieves." At home, we dry our tears and suddenly remember all the names: chocolate fudge, vanilla ice cream, milk shake, cotton candy. If we had a phone, we would call Mrs. Q., but we don't. Instead, we look out the window and sigh.

Mrs. Q. is a plump woman of Scottish descent, with sand-colored hair usually full of curlers. She always wears a bluish raggedy apron, and her purple lipstick only covers half of her mouth and two of her front teeth. She has a high-pitched broken voice, which calls her husband's name, "Hooooraaace ... ," but Horace never shows up. He only answers at her third call, and then with a hoarse voice, coughing and spitting tobacco. He is either very shy or doesn't care much for his wife; his pipe and can of beer is all he asks for.

We don't ask for much either. All we ask for is to see the world beyond this screen. But we never will, we know it. How could we, since we are nothing but characters in a book?

No One's Story

One Monday morning I went to the apartment complex's laundry room with a basket full of dirty clothes, put them in the machine, turned the machine on, and then realized I wasn't alone in there, as I had initially thought. No One was there. It was leaning against the vending machine, with a blasé air and a hollow body, moving its papery lips without producing any sound. Its speech was a waterfall of tumbling words that threatened to swallow everything in their vortex, yet I couldn't hear a single word. What was it saying that was so important, but couldn't make itself heard? The washing machine was also tumbling and gargling, its boisterous noise coiled around No One's story. I couldn't tell whether No One's story was the same one as that of the washing machine, but their words were impossible to separate. This is No One's story as I remember it:

I wish I could tell a tale full of so much detail that I would become entangled in its lateral detours and my heart would split apart like a red melon with small black seeds inside entirely identical to the plastic black seeds I once bought at Wal-Mart in the gardening department guided by a friendly clerk with a lemony smile who was watering the plastic seeds which are now in a wooden bowl in my living room and not inside a red melon which I wish I ate under a neon light with no one in sight.

When No One finished it was dark outside. Mexican housewives were coming and going in and out of the laundry room with baskets full of dirty clothes, as if to a river. The river could not be seen, but we could hear its far-away humming, and the grayness of its liquid body slipping over the pebbles hovered above the baskets of clothes. The housewives would empty the baskets into the washing machines, then leave, while other women of the same age and dark complexion would come in, take their clothes from the machines, and put them in the dryers, which were also humming, humming and tumbling, while far away the river kept flowing accompanied by No One's ceaseless murmur. When one of the women would open one of the washing machines, clothes of gaudy colors would jump out of it, purple, yellow, violet shirts with polka dots, checkered shorts, striped pants, and T-shirts with the American flag, and far away the river would grow darker and darker, while No One's story flowed alongside the walls, forever filling the now empty washing machines. The darker the river, the brighter the colors.

The Experimenter In Feeling

Others are experimenters in fiction. They experiment with words, silences, and then again, more words. I—I am an experimenter in feeling. That is, I feel as an experiment. Feelings—all kinds, the stronger the better: passion, jealousy, rage, pity, compassion, greed, joy, hate, love—I experience them all, one by one, like beautiful disposable necklaces. Each night, in front of the mirror, I take off another one and carefully lay it down in a box of burgundy velvet; and each morning, in front of the same mirror, I put on another one, after I carefully retrieve it from the same box. I wear my feelings on my sleeve. Sometimes I wear them hanging from my earlobes, like big round earrings of sterling silver, and I shake my head to hear their glassy jingle. "Glassy," like glass, which reminds me of the French *glas* with its vowel like a church bell, and which actually means "knell." Or of the Romanian *glas*, whose meaning is "voice." My feelings have a voice of glass. The mourning voice of a funeral knell. They mourn their own absence.

Once, following the advice of an aunt of mine, I went to a feelings doctor, and he gave me some pills to take, in the morning, at noon, and at night. Hope for breakfast, resilience for lunch, and despair at dinner. I asked what's the point when I can have despair at any time with no pills at all. Yes, he said, but if it comes in pills and with a proper dosage, you'll feel better.

I do, but it costs me a lot. When I mentioned it to the doctor, he said, a little exasperated by my skepticism, don't you see, it's *because* the price is so high that you feel better. The man has an answer for everything. I guess that's why they call him a doctor.

There is one problem with the pills, though. They interfere with my experiments in feeling.

"despair has four pairs of legs four pairs of aerial volcanic absorbent symmetrical legs."

My despair must have ten pairs of legs. But, of course, this is only a sentence, and a sentence has no legs at all.

Once, I tried to attach little legs to every single sentence, and by the time I finished, the page had walked away. That's why walking should be reserved exclusively for people. When they walk away it's because they have legs. On the other hand, when sentences walk away, it's because someone has mistaken them for people.

How could someone be such an idiot, I'm asking. A sentence is a sentence, and people are people. The first can be read, the latter read. The first moves horizontally (unless it's in Japanese), the latter vertically. The first is black on white, the latter come in many colors: black, white, and anything in between.

Really, how can someone mistake sentences for people? There's no more common sense these days. I once knew a guy who thought his head was a sentence. He kept looking for the predicate but could only find subjects—multiple personality disorder, the doctors said. In the end he killed himself—a bullet straight through his head—and when he died, they discovered the predicate hidden in the bullet. Well, it was predictable ...

The best thing about feelings is that they can't be put into words. Yet people do it all the time, completely oblivious of hurting feelings' feelings. If I were a feeling and someone put me into words, I would jump off the page and bite his nose. Maybe that's why so many good writers have such ugly noses. One can tell a writer just from his nose. Have you seen ... what's-her-name's nose ... the one who played Virginia Woolf in *The Hours*? Nicole Kidman. A kitten's nose. No nose at all. On the other hand, Virginia Woolf *has a nose*.

If I were a writer's nose and a feeling bit me, I would know better next time and stop sniffing around. But writers never learn anything from experience. As a matter of fact, no one learns anything from experience. That's why it may be better for all of us to stop experiencing anything and simply keep our feelings in a box of burgundy velvet, as a trophy of our former human existence.

The Missing Hand

When the furniture began to sweat, I knew that the world I'd known until then was gone. I tried to touch it with my fingers to convince myself that it was only an illusion, but as soon as my extended hand got close to it, the furniture drifted away, leaving me with my hand in the air like a beggar in the street. Everything around me was drifting away, recoiling before my touch in the powdery cloud of a crushed reality. Reality was being ground as if by a food processor. The gods had been turned into cooks with white aprons stooping over stews where the past simmered, and we were the spices.

Once, my hand got stuck in the reality grinder, and I couldn't get it back. I wondered if I could descend in the underworld like Orpheus searching for Eurydice, but there was no one to show me the way. "The underworld." How easy we toss around words with the irresponsibility of a child playing with a toy! What do I know about "the underworld?" Of course it was not the underworld. Just another world. But it was a world entirely separate from this one, and so far away that the mere thought of it brings tears to my eyes. I couldn't bring my hand back.

In that other world, my hand of salt melted at the touch of the things of snow. It melted and melted and melted, and I could only watch, helpless. I was cold, and wanted to blow into my cupped palms to warm them up, but I remembered I was missing one hand. Was there any relationship between the sweating furniture and my missing hand? I wondered. Would the sweating stop if I could bring my hand back?

I don't know if you ever lost a hand, but the feeling is one of complete aloneness, of a loneliness so raw that your very skin seems an insuperable wall cutting you off from the world. Behind that wall I coiled, looking around with eyes wide open; who knows, maybe my hand would show up.

Then, it began to rain. The rain was making a rattling sound as if it were hitting something on the ground, so I looked closer. Indeed, there was a heap of bare bones lying under the torrential rain. They seemed so lost, there in the open field with no roof in sight, and I felt sorry for them. I thought of my hand, which was probably at that very moment lost in another open field under who knows what skies and rains. I wanted to say a prayer for it—for *them*—but I remembered I didn't know any.

Stubborn Memory

When scientists discovered a way of erasing memory, people whose pasts were tainted by various traumas flocked to hospitals so that they could be reborn, free of the painful knots that gripped their souls.

One such man was a survivor of a concentration camp, a man who had spent his entire life reliving the horrors of his years in the camp. He was a man who didn't have much; as a matter of fact, the only thing he had was his memory, but he was willing to give up even that, just so he could find some peace in the few years left for him to live. The doctors did the procedure, after which the man went home, and for the first time in his life he could breathe without feeling the usual knot in his chest.

Not long after that he was called as a witness in a trial involving a former torturer from the concentration camp he'd been to. He was asked if he could recall the torturer, and he said no; if he remembered the pain that was inflicted upon him in the camp, the unspeakable tortures, the hunger, the humiliation, and he said no each time. He was given a vivid account of what he had gone through, but could remember none of it. On the way home, his old chest pangs came back, and he couldn't stop thinking about what he had just found: his past. He thought about it over and over again, he imagined himself in the camp with the other prisoners, and the man he saw at the trial as his guardian. Then he bought books and magazines dealing with the subject, and read articles about the horrors of similar camps and testimonies of survivors. He kept imagining. At night he had nightmares and during daytime, visions. He felt that he had lived all those things described and, claiming he had recovered his memory, he wanted to retract his former testimony and give a new one. But all the doctors and scientists said that it was practically and scientifically impossible for him to recover what has been erased, and that very likely our man had simply put together an imagined past out of images taken from books and other people's descriptions.

The man was by now so tormented that he decided once again to have his painful memories removed. The procedure was, once again, successful. But the judge in the trial of the former torturer said that, since a "non-memory" couldn't be erased, the successful erasure of the painful memories meant that the man actually *remembered*, and he condemned the torturer to many years of prison. The story made big headlines in all the papers, and some of them gave a detailed biography of the man-with-no-memory. And each time he read a new article, his past came before his eyes, hitting him again and again, and his memory kept coming back, like a wave slowly eating into a shore ...

The Girl in The Hat

For Joseph Cornell

She was born on All Saints' Day, at five thirty pm, in a black fedora hat. Somehow, after having made black and white pigeons appear, and gray rabbits with pink ribbons, the magician got confused and produced a little baby girl with a dark red, wrinkled face, and a violet throat shaken by spasmodic cries. The name they gave her—Bunny—didn't change a bit her so unbunny nature. In truth, nothing could change her. She was as unchangeable as Destiny, though she did not have one. She had no destination, she was destitute. Did she deserve more? Hard to say.

When she knocked at the wooden door atop the black marble stairs, and when, at the maid's welcoming gesture, entered the house with high ceilings, then the living room where, to pass the time, she began to observe the art on the walls and stayed in long contemplation before a box with red lobsters enclosed in what seemed to be an aquarium and a dinner table at the same time, she realized that there was much more to life than a black fedora hat and a gray rabbit with a pink ribbon. As she thought this, the door opened and a young man with a lobster face and pigeon neck came in. He wore a tailcoat with checkered pajama bottoms, and when he spoke, he seemed torn in two opposite directions, one following his formal coat, the other, his casual bottoms. "This will be fun," the Girl thought, and asked for a fork, a knife, and a plate with boiled lobsters. The expression of the lobster-faced man remained unchanged; in a soft voice he said something to the maid, who disappeared and returned minutes later with a big cardboard box. "This is for you," she told the Girl, who, after looking for a sign of approval in the young man's eyes and not seeing it, entered the big box and took the crossed-legged yoga pose.

The man began to laugh. "Who's the lobster *now*?" he said, full of malice, and the Girl had to bite her lips not to answer. "This won't get you anywhere," she said, and at this, the man seemed a little puzzled, then, seemingly in agreement with the Girl, opened the box and let her out. She took in a good breath of air, then remarked, "It's your turn now." At first, the man didn't understand, then, seeing her gaze at the box, was at a loss for words. "It's too small for me," he whispered. "Nonsense," the Girl said. "Just try."

While the Girl and the young man conversed in the living room, the maid and a male servant were engaged in something similar in the adjacent room. The maid had taken off her white, starched apron and placed it at the man's neck like a bib. He then proceeded to utter some very strange sounds, some resembling baby talk, others animal cries, while the maid laughed with her mouth wide open, a hand on her stomach. Suddenly an unseen hand slammed the door wide open and the Girl rushed out, a red lobster under her right arm. As she passed by, her own face bore an uncanny resemblance to the lobster, and her arms grew so long she had to tie them around her neck like a scarf.

After she exited the building, followed by the maid's broken laughter, the Girl couldn't rid herself of the maid's laughing face, of her bright white teeth insolently showing in her smooth, round baby face. The image of the teeth instantaneously brought to mind other teeth, her Grandmother's, the only thing left of the deceased woman. When her Grandmother spoke, her teeth occupied the entire room, glowing in the dark like a secret wrapped in tinfoil. Sometimes it was the teeth themselves that did the speaking, and the Grandmother just stood there following their movements with intense concentration, trying not to belch or pass wind. "Where did you get your teeth from?" people would ask at times, and she would laugh and shrug her shoulders, "Where could I have gotten them from? Well, the wolf, of course."

Grandma was very funny. Sometimes she cooked pies for days at a time, rhubarb pie, pecan pie, ricotta pie, even shepherd's pie, but this, no one ate. She just made it and pressed it between a book's pages like a flower, and said it was a shepherd's bookmark, but no one laughed. Except the Girl. But the Girl's laughter resembled gravel hitting the pavement in a storm. She literally collected it—that is, the gravel—in a box out of which she had once come out lobster-faced, but that was a long time ago. That was when Grandma was still alive, and her pies sold at the market on Wednesdays and Saturdays, and they had so many customers that they could buy dessert twice a week. Once, they ate so much custard they had to take Grandma to the hospital: her face was the color of mustard and they thought she was gone. Oh, they didn't know Grandma! No one did. Was she the bearded lady with knitted brown hats feeding the neighbors' cats pot stickers, chocolate pot de crème, and pot? Or was she the smelly old hag who talked to herself, smoked Cuban cigars, and hung out with the boys from Kmart? Or maybe her soul had migrated into the Girl born in a black fedora hat, and what she had endured as a hatless young girl was redeemed by a granddaughter who would turn out to be a lobster, sad as a lobster coming out of a box. Truth be told, this Girl was so sad even a lobster seemed happy by comparison. Even the box seemed happier, not to mention the hat. And the pen I am holding in my hand right now, which encloses in it this Sad Girl, is itself, if not a lobster, at least a crab moving backwards to the origins of sadness, a sorrowed pen whose rabbits are chewing bitterness in a black fedora hat adorning my head at this very moment, the head of a fool, a Crazy Grandma, an impotent rabbit—a disgrace to his fecund race—a pigeon eaten by rabies, a Sad Girl eaten by a pen, such a Sad Girl even the pen was struck dumb, so it had to stop.

The Garbage Woman

When she was little and people asked her what she wanted to be when she grew up, she'd answer, "a garbage woman," and their puzzled looks made her even prouder of her choice. She had nothing but spite for those snotty little brats with their sparkling toys and syrupy desires—doctors, teachers, engineers, dancers. No, she wanted to be a garbage woman. A garbage woman? The teacher repeated, incredulous, as her classmates giggled, exchanging glances. A garbage woman, she repeated. You mean, a cleaning lady, the teacher tried to clarify. No, a garbage woman. Well, I guess someone has to pick up the garbage, the teacher said, and everyone laughed. I won't pick up the garbage, she said. That's a garbage *man*. I will be a garbage *woman*. I will live with the garbage.

She had always been attracted to things close to the ground, little creatures and objects everyone stepped on, things no one noticed because they were invisible—snails, buttons, crumpled paper, various shells discarded after their contents had been eaten.

Sometimes she would lie on the ground with pieces of garbage all around, real garbage with a foul smell she found disgusting; yet, she wanted to become one with it, or rather to descend as low as garbage. Of course she realized that only years later. At the time she didn't think garbage was "low." She was instinctively drawn to it, as one is to one's own kind.

When, in her new country, she attempted for the first time to write the story of the garbage woman, it became the story of the baggage woman, a woman with a lot of baggage, carrying a huge suitcase made of unending sentences that descended coiled stairs into labyrinthine cellars and got drunk on the wine kept in rows of dusty bottles. At the time she had a boyfriend who was a little square, a chemist who didn't read much, but that didn't bother her. What bothered her was his wholesome handsomeness, his pretty-boy tanned face, broad shoulders, strong legs, and a general athletic demeanor breathing such health and positive thoughts that it made her want to throw up.

She was invited to give a reading and her boyfriend came along. She read from her story: *"The day I realized that not only my life could fit in a piece of baggage, but that I was that baggage, everything changed. 'Everything changed' is a way of speaking, for in fact, nothing changed around me, everything stayed the same, except for my baggage. I remember staring at it and trying to utter 'baggage,' but my ears heard again and again 'garbage, garbage.' I opened it and curled inside like a fetus. I imagined that someone would throw it into the sea and I would drift like that for weeks until the waves would bring it to the shore, and some bored tourist would spot it and say, 'Wow, look at this suitcase buried in the sand!' And he would open it, and I would jump out like a Jack-in-the-box, or better yet, I would sit still in a corner like a pearl inside its shell, and he would try to pull me out, but in vain. And then we would make a deal. 'Think of three wishes,' I'd say, 'and if I can guess, you can pull me out.' 'OK', he'd say, and I'd laugh to myself for he was going to lose either way. At any rate, all this was only in my head; no one threw the suitcase into the sea, so no one found it on the shore. But I began to live inside the suitcase and I knew that, now that I was a piece of baggage, very little separated me from being garbage, since a piece of baggage is something one usually puts on the ground and moves from place to place, something that comes and goes. I longed to be garbage."*

She raised her eyes and saw her boyfriend, who seemed much smaller than usual, with his head lowered as if trying to disappear under the chair, as if, yes, wanting to be garbage. For the first time, she felt a surge of tenderness for him and smiled in his direction. He didn't seem to notice or, if he did, let nothing show. After the reading, he stood aside, studying with concentrated attention the art on the walls until almost everyone had left and, save for the people putting the chairs away, they were alone. They went to a restaurant and for the entire course of the meal he sat silent, masticating pensively—if such a word could be applied to him—and avoiding her eyes. He barely touched his food, while she on the other hand gulped up everything, and at the end asked for a crème brûlée and a pomegranate pie. He watched her, as the desserts quickly disappeared from her plate, and when the waiter left with his credit card, he uttered, expelling the syllables with the care one would take in a theater audition, "I can't continue to go out with someone who wants to be a garbage woman. I have my pride!"

The word struck her in a bizarre way—"pride!" She remembered the first time she'd heard it. At the time she was probably eleven, twelve at most, and she was in one of those summer camps, but not for scouting, for mathematics. Communist regimes were in love with mathematics, so the children were fed big spoonfuls of it—food was anyway scarce—several times a day. As always, she didn't make any friends and spent her time noticing the allegiances that were being made and unmade. Sometimes she amused herself by trailing a group of girls who always whispered in each other's ears and giggled, then looked around to see if anyone was taking notice. One day they saw her, and began to laugh and whisper again.

"Where did you get those shoes?" one of them asked, and they all laughed again. She looked at her red, patent leather shoes and shrugged her shoulders, "I don't know, some store. Why?" "Because we want to get some too," and they exploded in a series of uncontrollable laughs that lasted about five minutes, after which they turned their backs on her and continued their stroll, whispering and giggling. But a little later, one of them turned around to pick up something that had fallen, and there she was, standing behind them with her red patent leather shoes and green dress with orange polka dots.

"Why are you following us?" Again, she shrugged her shoulders. "Get lost! Can't you see we don't like you?" "I won't bother you. I just want to be around you." "Don't you have any pride?"

The question almost made her lose her balance because she had to stop and think deeply, and then admit that no, she had no pride. She sat down on a rock covered with green moss, and by now the girls were far away and their giggles had vanished. All you could hear was the birds' chirping and the very light rustling of the surrounding vegetation. She contemplated her palm as if the word signifying the thing she didn't have was there. If she managed to pin the word down, would it be possible then to capture the thing? She closed her palm into a fist, holding the word captive. Then slowly, she brought her fist close to her mouth, and opening it only a crack, let the word slip into her mouth. Then she waited. She waited until sunset, when the ghostlike shadows among the trees chased her back to the camp, and when she got there, breathless, she knew that nothing had changed, and she still had no pride.

Maybe it all started when her elementary school teacher, a neurotic woman with freckles who still gave her nightmares thirty years later, came up with the devilish idea of sending them to clean up the school courtyard as punishment for misbehavior. As it happens, she was usually pretty well behaved, but bored to death during the long, slow hours moving like a caravan of ants with sacks on their backs. She began to do what it took to be sent out, and from then on she spent more time picking up garbage in the courtyard than with her classmates. The courtyard was vast and there was plenty to pick up: apple cores, tinfoil, paper airplanes, crumpled paper, and every once in a while a dirty feminine pad, or rather a cotton ball, since pads didn't exist at the time. Later, when she was at the age of using cotton balls, these disappeared too, and women used rags. This, and the lack of soap, toilet paper, water, deodorant, and toothpaste kept people in constant touch with an immemorial past—the past of the colorful, aromatic ages before the word "hygiene" existed.

The nine-year-old girl, who doesn't speak a word of English, has no idea that one day she'll live in a country where people take showers and change their clothes every day. She has no idea that one day she'll write of all this in English, though she has read several books by English authors and knows what a governess is, and thinks that if she doesn't grow up to be a garbage woman, then she'll be a governess like Jane Eyre. She would teach the master's pretty girls French language and literature, and when they attended balls, she would hide in a corner while they danced and sparkled. The hall would shine with laughter, lights, and champagne glasses, but she would be there, in a corner, gray and anonymous, content to be a witness.

When the teacher heard this one, she seemed even less pleased than about the garbage woman. "Our Party and its General Secretary have eliminated servants and the people's exploitation by the capitalist scum." She took a pen and the girl's gradebook, turned the pages at the end and scribbled under the column "Notes," "Your daughter needs to work on her revolutionary consciousness."

On her way back, the girl took out the gradebook and, after reading the sentence over and over, took a pen from her pencil case—whose story, that is, the story of the pencil case, is itself a gem, which shall be told a little further on—crossed the words "revolutionary consciousness" and replaced them with "cautionary recklessness." That sounded much better. There was something about the letters in those words that made her want to play with them. She found a bench, sat down and went on: "reactionary carelessness," "conciliatory restlessness"... The game was thrilling, so she took it to a new level: "cosmic lotion revelation ... evocative revocation ... derogatory vocative ...

votive luscious spaciousness ... spandex dexterity ... disastrous expenditure ... pantless epidemic ..." Of course, all this was in her old country's language, not in English, but you get the idea.

(To return to the story of the pencil case: the same schoolteacher demanded that the children put each morning on the upper right corner of their desks the following objects, one on top of the other: a notebook wrapped in red paper with a white label on which the words "The Oak from Liars Village" were written in capitals, a gradebook, and a pencil case. It may be why, for many years, the girl couldn't think of a pencil case without automatically seeing a red notebook. In it, the children were supposed to write down a synopsis of the previous day's evening news, most of which were about "The Oak from Liars Village." The Oak was none other than the Dear Leader, General Secretary of the Communist Party, and Liars Village was the name of the village where he was from. Now, you probably think I am making this up, but if there is anything true in this story, this is it.)

There was a Spanish writer who immigrated to the United States during World War I, Felipe Alfau, who wrote two books, then, if one is to believe Enrique Vila-Matas, stopped writing "as a result of the distress of having learnt English." Once he learned English, he suddenly became aware of certain intricacies of language of which he had never thought before. Until then he had, like everyone else, taken things and the words that express them for granted, but this new language removed everything from its natural state, putting things in such an unstable position that he could no longer make a natural connection between a certain thing and its corresponding envelope of sounds. In short, English complicated things so much for him that he had to stop writing.

Well, for her it was exactly the opposite. She had tried to write in her mother tongue, but it was the natural connection between object and word that made writing impossible. Every word she put on the page seemed a betrayal. Of what, she couldn't tell, but every single word was an unbearable betrayal of something that shouldn't have been expressed in the first place, so she threw everything away. English made things a lot simpler. The fact that in English the story of the garbage woman became the story of the baggage woman not only didn't bother her, but it was the very thing that made writing possible.

No, she had no pride and no revolutionary consciousness, and, as she found out in the New World, she had no ... what do they call that? That funny thing everyone works so hard to have here? Yes, "self-esteem." Luckily, in America everything was easy, and if one wanted to improve one's self-esteem, one just had to buy a book—one among the thousands on such a topic—that told them how to improve their self-esteem. So, everybody was constantly improving their self-esteem, which, had she wanted to improve her self-esteem, would have put her in a big competition with everyone else. But no, her own self was already enough of a burden, and rather than struggling for so much esteem, she just wanted to descend as low as she could. Let the others go up, she would happily go down. She had made Robert Walser's words her own:

> *Were a wave to lift me and carry me to the heights, where power and prestige are predominant, I would destroy the circumstances that have favored me and hurl myself downwards, to the vile, insignificant darkness. Only in the lower regions am I able to breathe.*

So, she tried to spend as much time as possible in the lower regions, among garbage, hoping that one day she would become so insignificant that she would disappear. She convinced her boyfriend—the one who wanted to leave her because she harbored the dream of becoming a garbage woman—to stay, and he accepted under the condition that they would each be independent and, as he put it, "see other people," if they so desired. She said yes, and, with a funny smile on his face, he told her to think it over, but she assured him that she had nothing to think about.

Several days later she found him with another girl, kissing and frolicking on their living room couch. The girl seemed embarrassed, but he appeared simply annoyed at having been interrupted, and without trying to hide his annoyance, asked her why she had come earlier than he expected her. She apologized, telling them to ignore her; she would go to her room and they could go on. At this, he exploded, "Are you trying to be ironic?" She really wasn't. She just wanted to make them feel comfortable, but the effect was exactly the opposite, for he grew extremely irritated, and, after a brief discussion with the girl, the latter took off. When they were alone, he began to yell, but soon stopped, realizing he was arguing with no one. She really wasn't trying to prove anything, and once he understood that, he looked at her as if she were a piece of garbage—and here, she couldn't help feeling a slight triumph—and asked, "How low can you sink?" Oh, he didn't know her. She could sink much lower than that.

He began to grasp that two days later when he came home with the other girl, and she offered them her room, then took a flashlight and a book, and moved into the washing machine. In a certain way, living in the washing machine was against her lifelong dream, since the washing machine is the very negation of garbage; but, in another way, her new residence placed her closer to life's lower regions and to a center of darkness where she aspired to vanish some day.

Once or twice a day, depending on his mood, he would come with some leftovers, open the machine's top and slip the plate inside, without looking. Sometimes he would drop the food on her head by mistake, and then she was, once again, close to being garbage. But one night, the machine's top slammed open, and instead of the usual plate, she saw his arm and his big, hairy hand, which grabbed hers, and violently pulled her out.

"I don't know what game you're playing, but I'm not getting any pleasure out of it," he said. "You can go back to your room!"

"Where is the other girl?" she asked.

"She's gone." And without offering any explanation, he gave her a big package wrapped in golden foil with a shiny, curly ribbon: "This is for you."

"For me? A present?"

Not used to receiving presents, she unwrapped it feverishly, tearing the foil apart. She held the object in her hand, blinded by its beauty, teary-eyed.

"Oh, you shouldn't have! It's beautiful!"

"I thought you'd like it."

It was a bright orange sleeveless jacket for garbage men, but since there are no jackets for garbage women, it was good enough. She put it on and admired herself in the big mirror inside the wardrobe, and as she was doing that, he asked her to take her clothes off and leave only the jacket on. At her puzzled look, he explained that he would have preferred a nurse's uniform, but he wanted to humor her, so now it was her turn to please him. She was not one to like walking around naked—orange jacket or not—and, as she reluctantly contemplated his proposal, she suddenly remembered how in her childhood she and her closest girlfriends had gone through a phase in which they wrote long novels—*romans feuilletons* with characters whose life stories spanned generations—and she had come up with the idea of making her characters meet the characters from her friends' novels in a sort of in-between land uniting several separate universes, a fiction that spilled over its frame into the real world, trying to cross over into another fiction. She remembered this because she felt the impulse to throw him into another story, of giving him a kick right in the butt so he would fall over into the mirror and tumble down all the way to … to the world of the Unclean, as her grandmother used to say. She lingered a while around this word from the old language, moving it inside her mouth with the tip of her tongue, a word she had forgotten and which was coming back now in such an unexpected way. The Unclean. Peasants in her grandparents' village had many names for the Devil. "May-the-Church's-Gong-Kill-Him!" was another one. (The gong, used in the old days to call the monks and the nuns to their daily rituals, was still used during her childhood, in some old monasteries.) It was truly His name, and the peasants would say it really fast—a way of avoiding pronouncing the word itself, which would have summoned the evil spirit.

But as she thought of all this, it occurred to her that the Unclean wasn't a good place to send "him" to since the Unclean was linked to garbage, and she didn't want her garbage contaminated by his presence. Of course, she didn't mention any of this to him. Instead, she took her pants off, went to the kitchen to fetch a broom and returned butt naked, smiling in a way that attempted to be sexy. "Happy?" she asked. His face contorted in a grimace of disgust. Without an answer, he darted off, sma … sla … what was that word? Splashing the door!

It was a problem she still had with English. She often went to the chicken to put a kitchen in the oven, referred to men as "she" and to her female friends as "he," asked people not to sleep on her toes, got down the bus, slapped the door, smashed the potatoes, squashed the water, sweatened the cake, put on a sweeter when she went outside and took it down when she came inside, called her boyfriend "sweatie," and once, during her first year as a TA, asked a student called Weather what was the Heather like, and thirty mouths laughed, and she asked them to stop making funny and to restore their work, and then they went hysterical, and she walked out on the classroom, splashing the door.

After he left, she stood in the middle of the room trying to remember the words that best expressed what she felt. "That takes the cherry? No, it's something with a cake … That puts the cake on the Sundae!" And, after some additional thought, "That takes the cherry off the Sundae!"

Fried Brains

It was in the eighties. The store shelves were empty, the TV program had been reduced to two hours, which was all for the best since the power was out most of the time, days went by with no running water, and a wind so cold blew through the entire country that you just wanted to lie down in a coffin and be done with it. But it takes more than that to shut down the stubborn machinery known as the body, so people kept being alive, and occasionally even enjoyed it.

At Venus, the biggest restaurant in town, only one thing was left on the menu: fried brains. With the exception of graduation parties or some celebration of the local nomenklatura, the restaurant was empty all the time. That's why, after several weeks of excruciating boredom, Gigi, the eavesdropper hired by the Secret Police to keep an eye—or rather an ear—on the place, was very happy when a new customer showed up.

The customer ordered fried brains and, since there was nothing to listen to, Gigi followed his every move, not because he expected to discover anything, but simply not to lose his skills.

When the waiter brought the brains, the customer asked for a glass of wine and the waiter looked at him as if he had asked for a fried baby.

"We have no wine here," he said, indignant. "There is a sign in the window. It says, 'Customers should bring their own wine.'"

The customer said he would keep that in mind and next time he would come with his own wine. Indeed, the very next day he showed up at the same time as the day before, carrying a bottle of red wine. Again, he ordered fried brains. When he asked for bread, the waiter answered with the same indignation, "Didn't you see the sign in the window? It says, 'The customer should bring his own bread.' We have no bread!"

The next day, the man entered the restaurant with a bottle of wine and a loaf of bread. The restaurant was sunk in darkness, and the waiter explained that the power was out.

"The customer should bring two candles," he said.

The man ate in darkness, which made Gigi quite nervous because he couldn't see anything. The next day the man showed up with a bottle of wine, a loaf of bread and two candles. The waiter brought him the brains and everything seemed perfect. But, at the end of the meal, as the customer was picking his teeth with a toothpick, the waiter presented him with a broom: "The customer should sweep the room after eating."

So the man took the broom and performed as best as he could. When he arrived the next day, he was carrying—besides the bottle of wine, the loaf of bread, and the candles—a broom. The waiter gave him a yellow grin, "You think you're smart, don't you?"

"Just in case you are out of a broom," the man said.

"We are not out of a broom," the waiter replied. "We are out of fried brains."

"So what do you have?"

"Fried patience.[1] We have fried patience."

The waiter and the eavesdropper looked at each other jubilantly, wondering what the customer was going to do next.

---

[1] Romanian idiomatic expression meaning "nothing to eat."

But our man, who had been fed on fried patience for most of his life, was not one to lose his patience so easily. Very calmly, he took the flower vase from the table, hit himself in the head with all his strength and when he had made a little hole in it, he proceeded to pull out his brains onto the empty plate. Then, he fried them right in front of the two men, as they watched, incredulous.

"Are you out of your brains?" the eavesdropper yelled. "Why are you eating your brains?"

"Whose brains was I going to eat?" the man replied calmly, wiping his mouth with his sleeve, as there were no napkins. "If I ate yours, I'd get as dumb as a doorknob, and he—pointing at the waiter—must surely be out of them. I had no choice."

Uncle Otto Plays Chess

Uncle Otto plays chess late afternoons on Wednesdays and Fridays till almost midnight, and sometimes even after. His chess partner, his neighbor Gyuri, speaks Romanian with a thick Hungarian accent that seems to come out of his even thicker mustache. Uncle Otto knows only several Hungarian words, but, maybe out of deference for his guest, insists on using them with a frequency that makes Aunt Rajssa roll her eyes and give me conspiratorial glances. "*Nemsobot* (Don't) ... *Pirosz toiasz* (Red egg) ... *Te vogi* (You are) a dangerous fellow."

Gyuri, on the other hand, curses constantly, always sporting a wry smile, as if he were cajoling the local supermarket clerk to give him an extra pound of sugar. He mixes Romanian and Hungarian into an uninterrupted murmur that sounds something like this: "You, Son-of-a-Horse ... Are you trying to pull my bells? You've got some balls in that bald head of yours. Hey, what are you doing with my rook? Rook, rook, patapouk. You can't do this to me, comrade!"

No one knows what "patapouk" means—Gyuri has a penchant for making up words that rhyme. Uncle Otto sequesters Gyuri's rook, which he places on his side, sheepishly asking for forgiveness with that baby face of his. Meanwhile, Aunt Rajssa and Erzsi, Gyuri's wife, sip Turkish coffee, glancing from time to time at the two players. Erzsi talks about her new daughter-in-law, a short woman, half her son's height, I am not kidding you, when she looks at him she looks straight into his balls, he has to put her on a chair to kiss her, and she doesn't move a finger in the house, her mother didn't teach her a thing. A whore—Romanian no less.

"I thought you said she was a virgin," Aunt Rajssa interrupts. "Well, yes, yes, she was a virgin, but what kind of a virgin? You know, the whore slept for months with *my* Joska without letting him touch her. In the same bed!"

Gyuri turns his head at the sound of the raised pitch, which he has learned to ignore, but which sometimes, like now, reminds him of the whistle or the squeal of a train's brakes—the train he missed when he agreed forty years ago to marry her.

"Can you imagine what this must have done to my Joska? *My Joska?*" "He's not *your* Joska anymore, get over it!" Gyuri jumps in.

"Oh, she knew what she was doing, the whore," Erzsi goes on, unperturbed. I told him, "Joska dear, you don't need to get married, I'll give you everything, don't you have everything you need here? Everything you need! This woman can't even warm up a soup for you. When are you going to eat a warm soup now, Joska? Oh, Joska, don't leave your mother! She ... She ... She ... How do you say that in Romanian? She made him lose his pumpkin." "His head," Aunt Rajssa intervenes, dryly. "His head, his pumpkin, his balls," Gyuri says, patting his mustache and glancing meaningfully at Uncle Otto, who lowers his eyes, blushing. "You old, lecherous perv," Erzsi throws at Gyuri, who laughs, winking at her.

Uncle Otto wins again. He apologizes, but Gyuri dismisses him with a quick hand gesture, "You mother-plucker ..."

So what happened this Wednesday? Why didn't Gyuri come as usual? Why did Uncle Otto come home with a drooping face, and then whisper, seriously agitated, for almost two hours with Aunt Rajssa in the kitchen?

It turns out that Uncle Otto had been stopped on his way to the butcher shop by Mache, our building's informer—one of them, anyhow, the one everyone knows what he is up to. And he doesn't make much of an effort to hide it either. He had a cigarette butt in the corner of his mouth and a beret on his head—not your customary secret police officer outfit, but he is really low on the food chain, as they say. He was very friendly—"Hey, Otto, long time no see! Still painting?"—which put my uncle on his guard and made him even less communicative than he usually is. But he is not one to say no to a friendly invitation to a cup of coffee, or rather to our local coffee shop, where, in the crammed space full of standing bodies exhaling clouds of smoke through all of their visible holes, and not drinking coffee or tea because there never is anything to drink or eat, everyone has an opinion about the latest book release, and, in a lower voice, even about the Dear Leader. So it turns out, Uncle Otto later said, red with anger and pounding his fist on the table, that Mache wanted him to spy and inform on Gyuri. "Me!" Oh, nothing really major, just things like: does comrade Gyuri have healthy morals and principles, or is he likely to be seduced by this decadent stuff one see these days on videos? "We never talk politics, comrade Mache," Uncle Otto said, trying to appease him, "*never*. And I don't think Gyuri is one to watch videos. This stuff is for twenty-year-olds, not for people like us."

"Well, I'll see you next time, when you have more to tell me," comrade Mache said as they were parting, winking playfully and patting Uncle Otto on his shoulder.

Uncle Otto left confused, mumbling something under his breath and wondering whether comrade Mache's words meant that his name would henceforth be on some list next to hundreds of other names, and whether the presence of his name on that list meant that he was an informer or, on the contrary, an enemy of the people whose whereabouts should be carefully watched by other people from that or another list. He himself wasn't sure of what he had done, since each time comrade Mache mentioned Gyuri, he kept excusing himself, while at the same time nodding approvingly whenever comrade Mache said something about how, in spite of some small shortcomings, our nation was on its way toward the highest peaks of prosperity it has ever known. Sure, the stores were always empty and you couldn't get a cup of coffee in any café in town, he'd grant Uncle Otto that, but it was because our people ate and drank way too much. Whenever the stores were replenished, our fat, greedy people devoured everything in half an hour. Did Uncle Otto know that our people were the biggest consumers of bread in Europe? He didn't? Well, now he knew. What was that? Uncle Otto thinks that if the people had something else to eat besides bread, they would probably eat less bread? Ha! He thinks so? He has no idea how people are: you give them salami, and next thing you know, they'll ask for cheese.

Only late that night did we realize that Gyuri had failed to show up for his weekly portion of chess. How would he know that something was going on? Or rather, did he know anything? Uncle Otto, who was given to easy fits of crying, began to tear up, fearful that something irreparable and beyond his control had occurred.

The next day, Uncle Otto woke up early, placed himself behind the door, and waited until Gyuri came out of his apartment; then, he exited and "ran," as it were, into his neighbor.

"He *knows*," he said, when he returned minutes later with a newspaper under his arm. "He looked at me in this really funny way."

Aunt Rajssa told him that he was paranoid, that the only person who could have told Gyuri anything was comrade Mache, but that would have defeated the purpose of his entire enterprise. But when the following Wednesday came and Gyuri failed to show up again, we agreed that something was up. And so, on Thursday morning, Uncle Otto, in his fuzzy slippers with holes in the soles, and a burgundy robe of thick cotton, knocked shyly at Gyuri's door. The door opened and, before Uncle Otto could open his mouth, Gyuri, with a finger placed on his, closed the door behind him and invited himself into our apartment. "We can't talk at my place," he whispered. "I'm sure there are microphones."

"?"

"I have been contacted, you know … *They* asked me to do something."

"They did?"

"Yes," he paused dramatically, waiting to see the effect on Uncle Otto's face. "They want me to spy on you."

"*You?* On *me?*"

"Yes. *Me* on *you.*"

"Well, well …" Uncle Otto began to stammer. Was Gyuri setting him a trap? Was he testing him because he suspected something? Should he keep his mouth shut? Or should he tell him the truth? Maybe comrade Mache has asked them both to do the same thing—after all, it would be the only way for him to see if they were telling the truth.

"Well, this is so funny," Uncle Otto began, "because *they* have contacted me too."

"You?"

"Me."

"To spy on *me?*"

"Yes. *Me* on *you.*"

So Uncle Otto and Gyuri spent the rest of the day concocting a report filled with the things they didn't say on Wednesday when they didn't play chess, but they consented to claim they did so they could each, separately, present comrade Mache with a convincing picture of their weekly dialogue. For example, Uncle Otto did not say, "I wish my Serioja (his son) had a more advanced revolutionary consciousness and spent his time reflecting on the accomplishments of the Party and its Dear Leader, rather than waste his time dancing," but this was one of the sentences they agreed on. Nor did Gyuri say, "At night I have to drag my Erzsi from the TV because she savors every word of our Dear Leader and can't fall asleep until she hears one of his speeches," but they almost agreed on it, before deciding that it was too much and, gulping down another glass of *palinka*, suddenly inspired, Gyuri went on, "She gets horny like a bitch in heat, tears off her clothes, and throws her panties at the TV begging our Leader, who so wisely navigates our ship, to rock her boat too, to nail her down with the nail the degenerate bourgeoisie had hammered into his tongue when he was spreading communist manifestoes in his youth—remember the story they taught us in elementary school?—oh, my Erzsi is thirsty for some proletarian wisdom! And does she get it every night!" Here, Gyuri beat his chest emphatically, almost choking with laughter.

But comrade Mache wasn't born yesterday, do I look like I am green behind my ears or something? Uncle Otto had to acknowledge that no, he definitely didn't. He had arrived at the Arizona Crocodile Café ten minutes before the scheduled time only to spot, with a look of stupor on his face at the sight of his friend, standing in a corner, Gyuri—did I mention there were no chairs and everyone stood by a small, round, empty table? So, this is how it was: comrade Mache had invited them both to the café, *at the same time*. It certainly saved time and money. After the two neighbors reported on each other before a steaming cup of nothing matched by what everyone smoked at the time (that is, everyone who could afford something other than the local unfiltered cigarettes), a Kent cigarette, comrade Mache invited them to the Intercontinental, the fancy downtown restaurant whose only customers were the tourists and his colleagues in black leather jackets. There they had not only coffee—well, more like a brownish lukewarm liquid—but even our nationally famous fried brains.

"*You* had fried brains with comrade Mache?" Aunt Rajssa asked, incredulous.

"Yes, I did," Uncle Otto answered. "And Gyuri had two portions."

Gyuri also had too much wine, so when he later narrated the episode in Aunt Rajssa's small kitchen, he had to frequently interrupt himself, either because he was laughing too hard, or else his words became a bilingual mumbled gibberish. "I am a father too," comrade Mache supposedly said after browsing the reports brought by the two neighbors. "I can't feed my family with this silly bullshit of yours. Do you think comrade T is going to swallow any of this? We're going to do this together, all of us."

So all of them, together, worked an entire afternoon on the twin reports, one of comrade Otto on comrade Gyuri, the other of comrade Gyuri on comrade Otto.

From comrade Mache's *Report on his meeting with comrade Gyuri and comrade Otto at the Arizona Crocodile Café*

On Thursday, November 15, comrade Otto, comrade Gyuri and myself being at the Arizona Crocodile Café and having a friendly discussion initiated by me at Officer T's orders, comrade Gyuri disclosed that he had an obsession with cow patties, while at the beginning, comrade Otto didn't disclose anything, being reserved and very uncommunicative, which prompted comrade Gyuri to make several jokes about comrade Otto's wife, Rajssa, who, as appears from comrade Gyuri's allusions, is not very appreciative of our Party's and our Leader's accomplishments, having once said in the presence of comrade Gyuri that our Party can kiss her ass, and then comrade Otto replied visibly annoyed, But your Erzsi says that all the time, No, my Erzsi says that our Party can kiss her *Hungarian* ass, comrade Gyuri answered laughing and winking at me, which made me think that he must have heard the unfair gossip according to which I am Hungarian or even Jewish, which is entirely false, as my hundred percent Romanian name can attest to, so I said, comrade Gyuri, if this is how you want to play, we can change our tune too, and then he grew serious and engaged in a long explanation about how his wife, comrade Erzsi, is turned on whenever she sees our Dear Leader, but I didn't answer, thinking to myself that comrade Gyuri's wife's admiration for our Leader is not very flattering, she being fat as night and ugly as sin.

From comrade Otto's *Report on his meeting with comrade Gyuri and comrade Mache at the Arizona Crocodile Café*

On Thursday, November 15, comrade Mache, comrade Gyuri and myself were at Arizona Crocodile Café at comrade Mache's invitation. Comrade Mache took out a pack of Kent cigarettes and offered to share them. I refused. Comrade Gyuri took one (during the entire conversation he took a total of three cigarettes). Comrade Gyuri made a joke about how my wife, Rajssa, isn't as appreciative of the evening news as she appears to be of American movies, particularly love stories. The words he used were rather crude, so I won't repeat them here. I replied by saying that his wife, Erzsi, was an even bigger fan of American love stories, at which comrade Gyuri, suddenly irritated, burst out, "Are you calling my wife a chicken?" "I am not," I said, perplexed, not having any idea where in the world that came from. Comrade Mache seemed to find this very amusing, and added, "A plucked chicken." Now, comrade Gyuri attacked comrade Mache: "Are you calling my wife a plucked chicken?" "I am not," comrade Mache defended himself in turn. And added, "*He* is" (pointing at me). "I would never call anyone's wife a plucked chicken, let alone Erzsi, of whom I've always been very fond," I said, indignant. Comrade Mache raised his eyebrows, as if somebody had revealed something unexpected, and, puckering his lips: "Oh, la, la! What are we finding out? Comrade Otto … Comrade Gyuri … Comrades!" This was more than I could bear, so I told comrade Mache that I would not allow such uncalled-for insinuations, at which he replied, "Now, comrade Otto, this is no reason to take offense. Comrade Gyuri here has more reasons to get upset. Everyone knows that his wife, comrade Erzsi, and our Dear Leader are … how should I put this?" At this, comrade Gyuri told comrade Mache to go pluck himself, at which comrade Mache replied, "Hey, comrade Gyuri, we are going to change our tune. We can use other methods, you know."

From Comrade Gyuri's *Report on his meeting with comrade Otto and comrade Mache at the Intercontinental restaurant*

As we ate our fried brains with fries and drank our red wine, comrade Mache suddenly began to complain how sick he was of all this, of all the lies and the bullshit, and that whenever he saw our Dear Leader on the evening news, he felt the almost uncontrollable desire to throw a cow patty right between his eyebrows, imagining how the melted patty would trickle into his mouth.

I knew it was a provocation, and at first I didn't want to answer, but then I realized that the whole point of us being there was to report on our shortcomings and ideological failures, so I had to oblige because otherwise what would even be the point of writing this report?

I laughed, "That's exactly what I think when I watch the news," and comrade Mache patted my right shoulder in male solidarity, accidentally hitting the wine bottle and causing it to spill its red guts on the white tablecloth, so he asked the waiter to bring another bottle—the third one—and then asked comrade Otto what *he* thought when he watched the news, and he answered that he didn't think much because it is not the job of the proletarian class to think, but were he to think, he would think exactly what everyone else thought. At this, comrade Mache, whose mouth had been stretched all the way up to his ears till then, stopped laughing: "Are you pulling my leg?" "Me?" "Yes, you." "No, Sir, I am not." "Sir?!" he said, his face red with anger. "Sir?! Do you think we are in the United f ... States of America? There are no 'sirs' here, comrade." Comrade Otto apologized and comrade Mache calmed down, so we went back to work on our report.

Report to Comrade T on Comrade Mache's Meeting with Comrade Otto and Comrade Gyuri at the Intercontinental Restaurant

After a cordial and fruitful discussion in spite of the clouds of smoke at the Arizona Crocodile Café whose name is a testimony to the wit of our people who first christened it "Arizona" as a reference to the deserted or rather empty shelves though some people say it refers to the long empty conversations our citizens particularly the students and the parasites i.e. the unemployed writers and artists have and at some point someone added "crocodile" and it stuck

After as I said a cordial and fruitful discussion comrade Otto comrade Gyuri and myself left that foggy rat hole and migrated to the warmer and more welcoming restaurant where the members of our profession enjoy spending most of their time the Intercontinental. My favorite waiter Gica was there so before we even ordered he came with a bottle of red wine and but what am I talking about suffice it to say that as I was opening my ears and closing my zipper comrade Gyuri opened his mouth and proceeded to throw in it peppers sausages red and white stuffed cabbage meatballs as if there was no tomorrow

Isn't comrade Erzsi going to be upset if you come home ten pounds heavier than when you left I said as Gica opened the second bottle of wine and Gyuri increasingly communicative began to tell us how when he was in college every night he and his roommates made jokes—oh the kind of jokes you couldn't tell your sister jokes that would make your ears wilt if they were flowers—about the Dear Leader but when the Dear Leader came to visit his sorry excuse for a town and everyone was waiting on the sidewalk he says I began to applaud like everyone else though I hated his guts go figure I sometimes think that's how we all are like sheep

I said that's what you think it's good to know and you comrade Otto Oh *I don't think* comrade Mache he said I know better than to think I stopped that a long time ago and by then we were at the third bottle or I guess fourth which is the bottle we are drinking now as I what am I doing here Gica whenwhatwe are as we are right or rather writing this no matter what they say our people isn't dumb how can they be dumb if our Leader is so smart? That's what I think for though I drink I still think who said that Pascal or someone

With all due respect comrade I think that's Othello Gyuri said What are you talking about I replied You think that because I am a man of the people I don't know who Othello is With all due respect comrade Otto intervened Gyuri means no disrespect but he reads a lot I'm telling you it's Othello Gyuri repeated and added emphatically I think therefore I drink Idiot I said everyone knows that Othello is famous for Et tu Desdemona which means You too Desdemona Do you know who Desdemona was comrade Otto?

I'm afraid I don't read this kind of stuff Comrade Otto answered But when I was little my mother used to call me Othello you know as a pet name Now this is too good Gyuri exclaimed Comrade Otto-Othello Ha ha this is too good comrade Othello And I had to stop him and explain to comrade Otto who Desdemona was and what a jealous fellow Othello was you know that's why I don't understand jealousy like that that's what I told them at the House of Culture when the students were rehearsing the play the other day comrades jealousy is a bourgeois feeling we can't allow this kind of

What? Another bottle? Bring it on. Rope it big nope trink gone what nottle ring and ring not a thing rip and dip the meek shall inherit the earth who said that Dear Leader tic tic tic tac tac tac the clock is going down the drain your nose has a beautiful color for a corpse drip drip drip someone is going down the drain or as they say in our beautiful language everything is drifting on Saturday's waters everything must come to an
end

Twin Sisters

> "The action of this story will result in my transfiguration into someone else and in my ultimate materialization into an object."
> CLARICE LISPECTOR

> "[...] a deathlike sleep beside a girl put into a sleep like death."
> YASUNARI KAWABATA

Our lives are defined by the loss we experience in our youth. We are our loss and go through life trying to drape in a shirt of light our soul's dark night at the bottom of which lie buried our past selves. If we lost a father, we will look for him in all our future loves; if we lost a friend, all our friendships will bear the mark of that bond; if we lost a sister, we will try to recreate ourselves in the image of the lost one. But if we lost our double, which is the secret, invisible quest of our lives, life will become for us the mere shadow of an unattainable universe called "the real," and we will spend our lives trying to unravel behind each laugh, its valley of tears, behind each I, the faceless grip of nameless lack of being.

I lost my twin sister, Hilda, at birth. I was told about it when I was five or so, but I remember clearly that even before that I used to be in constant dialogue with an imaginary double, who, I knew, was my sister. My parents' revelation put only a name on the shapeless longing I always felt. They never told me to keep it a secret, but something inside me told me that, of all the layers to be found in my being, the secret of my double should be the last thing to be discovered.

Nowadays, everyone wants to shed their secrets, preferably under a huge electric light in front of an audience that will gasp and sigh in empathy, mouths dribbling with excitement, blood rushing in their numb veins. But for the mystery of one's existence, for that which cannot be shown nor shared, the masters of the spectacle that passes for life have no use.

All the stories I read in my childhood were stories of orphans—*The Adventures of Oliver Twist*, *Jane Eyre*, *Tom Sawyer*, fairy tales with the good and the evil sister, the good and the evil brother. I secretly knew that the story of the orphan is the story of the last one who one day will be the first, the ancient story of *the prince and the pauper*, and I thought of myself as orphaned by my sister. Besides, the story of the orphan is always intertwined with that of the lost brother or sister. Even later in life, when I read Simone de Beauvoir's *Memoirs of a Dutiful Daughter*, what interested me were not the saltless details about her meeting with Sartre, but her friendship with the mysterious Zaza, her double, who was everything she wasn't: charming, spontaneous, the fascinating I fated to die when she, Simone, was entering life.

I was a solitary child and an even more solitary adolescent. Other children's gregarious energy scared me; boys, especially, represented a form of life made of tense muscles and sordid violence. But if young men seemed all in various degrees the exact opposite of the spirit, older men were an entirely different breed. Was it because Jane Eyre's lover was twenty years older than she? Or was it because the orphan girl was fated to find the lover and the father in one and the same person?

Never did I feel more an orphan than when I reached sixteen. It was the age when my parents had promised that I would be allowed to walk to the edge of the forest, and I didn't wait long for it. One summer afternoon, I slipped out of the house, and to the forest! I knew exactly what I was looking for, our new neighbor's much talked about house. The house was as I expected: big, gray and of an old, imposing stone that contrasted with the green, luxurious vegetation around.

A poorly dressed woman opened the door, no doubt the cook or the maid, her mouth stretched into a yawn so big it took her a whole minute to ask what I wanted. I answered I wished to see the lady of the house, and she said, "Alda?"

I said, "Yes," then she disappeared. After several minutes, a man in his mid-forties came and said that his daughter was asleep, but I could wait in her room until she woke up. I crossed the threshold, thinking that, through a slight change of events, I could have been born in that home, with a father dressed in an impeccable dark suit, lazily sucking on a pipe while reading the daily paper. I entered Alda's room and felt I had stepped into a space meant to preserve silence, as if it were an object to store in a cabinet. Everything was white—the quilts, the rugs, the curtains, the wooden furniture—and the rugs' softness under my feet absorbed the sun's rays, enclosing them in its whiteness.

Alda lay asleep in a king-size bed that occupied about a fourth of the room. She too was dressed in a white lace nightgown and her brown hair was spread on the pillow. It was big and fluffy, the kind of pillow I always wanted but never had because my mother believed in austerity. Several other big fluffy pillows were spread on the bed. An aroma of mixed flavors lingered in the room, a mixture of cinnamon and Indian spices, the kind that might come from some incense. I began to look around with the joy that other people's homes usually give me; I opened all the drawers and browsed various photo albums full of pictures from Alda's childhood, looked at her collection of plush animals, inspected her dozens of pairs of white lace underwear, opened a diary, read several lines, put it away, touched her dolls, which were lined up in ascendant order, from very small to very tall, opened her Russian dolls and then put them back.

The grandfather clock on the wall struck five with such suddenness and in such a low, somber tone that I stopped in the middle of my gesture and quickly moved to a neutral spot in the center of the room. There I sat on the rug and waited. Alda gave out a moan, turned on one side, then the other, as if she were about to wake up, then she went to sleep again. I sat there for half an hour, and at exactly five-thirty, Alda opened her eyes with no preliminary warning, saw me and asked in a clear voice:

"Who are you?"

"I am your neighbor," I said. "Your father told me to wait here until you woke up."

She measured me with restrained curiosity, and I could see, when she laid her eyes on me, that they were unusually elongated and of an intense dark blue with a metallic coldness in them. Her hair was even longer than mine, almost to the waist and its heaviness made her head tilt to one side. She put on a velvety white gown and slippers and asked me to follow her.

In the living room, Alda's father, who apparently had been reading his newspaper all this time, didn't seem surprised to see us and invited me to sit down. None of them seemed to have any curiosity about me or where I had come from, and Alda asked in a matter-of-fact voice if I cared to join them in a game of Scrabble. I said, "I love Scrabble," putting a little more excitement in this than might have been necessary, and I saw Alda's smile at the corners of her lips. Next to her father, she seemed his exact replica, only of a different gender: they had the same tanned, smooth skin, the same wavy hair, though his was receding, the same dark blue eyes, and most of all, an unsettling voice with a haunting quality to it, almost masculine in Alda's case, but feminine in its trembling inflections. They were talking to each other as if I were not there, and when their eyes met a secret seemed to pass between them, of which I was not a part. The father had the same ironic, detached smile as the daughter, and while playing, he kept his pipe in his mouth. At one point, he passed it to her and she took a good pull, then handed it to me. I made a shy sign of refusal, and both of them burst out laughing.

After I left, their faces and voices accompanied me all the way back home. And suddenly I stopped, full of the realization that their smile, the way they looked into each other's eyes, was that of lovers.

At night I dreamed of a well with dark blue water into which I looked fascinated as if into an enormous eye, drawn to it by a nameless, impersonal force, and the closer I got to it, the more I could feel the presence of my sister Hilda. I woke up, bathed in sweat, with the voice of my sister rhythmically beating in my ear.

The next time I went to Alda's house, I scrutinized the maid's face, hoping to find in it a sign that would explain her employers' behavior, but the only visible thing was the same ironic smile. The whole house was sunk in a deep quiet, an abnormal and foreboding one, with not even a creak of furniture. After letting me in, the maid told me that both Alda and her father were asleep. Then, smiling, she took me to the father's room, where he lay in a huge bed, with the appearance of one who is deeply asleep. And after that, she took me by the hand to show me Alda's room—the same one I had been in last time, where Alda, as in my previous visit, was sleeping in the same white bed. Her tan seemed to have faded, and the smell of incense was replaced by a faint, sweet perfume that dominated the room, but when I got closer to the bed, I sensed coming from it a smell of milk and baby skin. Alda's face radiated such peacefulness that she seemed to recede into an unreachable space of sweetness, dreamless and devoid of feeling.

"Would you like to play a game of Scrabble until she gets up?" asked the maid, and without waiting for my answer, she laid the game on the white rug. I joined her and for a while we played in silence.

"Why is Alda sleeping so much?" I asked suddenly, thinking that if I took her by surprise, she wouldn't have time to make up a lie. But she answered right away, without showing the slightest concern.

"Alda hates reality. She thinks that the real is a prison for people with no imagination. So each afternoon I give her a medicine that puts her into a deep sleep. It is a sleep like death—or so she told me, because I never tried it—and each time, she wakes from it with a sense that life has just started. You should try it sometime ..."

"Why don't *you* try it?" I answered back.

"Oh, me," she said mockingly. "I love reality. I have no imagination."

When the clock struck five, Alda began to toss and moan, flipping a hand as if chasing a shadow or a bee.

"She'll be up in no time," the maid said.

And so she was. This time, she paid even less attention to my presence than the last time, but she invited me nevertheless to join her and her father in the living room. He was waiting for us, wrapped in a long dark blue gown, shuffling his feet with his eyes half open, spreading a glow of sleep and absentmindedness that stuck to everything he touched. Of all the eyes present in the room, none met—gazing was relegated here to a very light, feathery contact between the eye and what met the eye. Alda herself kept yawning, albeit discreetly, and trying to hide it behind the same hand that had been chasing shadows and bees a minute ago.

I thought of a honey-glazed universe and I suddenly longed for the sleeping potion that was keeping them in this state of lightness and oblivion. They played chess and I watched. Their hands moved with mathematical precision, making and unmaking the battlefield, but their eyes looked past each other, like those of blind people. The more I looked at them, the more I wanted to be part of their non-presence. At the end of the game, Alda invited me to come next Wednesday, with a tone that made it clear I was to stay away for the rest of the week.

At home, I too began to move like a person only half of this world, but for different reasons: I couldn't sleep. I kept thinking of the two of them, her likeness covering the face of my sister whenever I fell asleep, and his voice slipping through the narrow gate that separated my dream from the real. It is during these days that I began to regard with suspicion what people call "love." I realized that one can fall in love with an image and even with a voice, but what is an image and what is a voice? Do they really exist, in the same sense that a table or a chair exist? Isn't the image the untouchable copy of the real, and isn't the voice, the untouchable vibration of *something* we can hear in reality? We see the image and we hear the voice, but they don't exist. Does *a person* even exist?

I ruminated these things over and over until Wednesday came. This time I showed up earlier, but the maid didn't seem surprised. Nothing seemed to faze her.

I said, "I want the medicine." Her ironic smile bordered on mockery, but she remained silent.

So I drank it. It was tasteless and odorless, like sleep. After I drank it, she took me to Alda's room, helped me undress and put on a white lace nightgown, then I lay next to Alda. The same smell of milk hit me again, but this time it was coming not only from her, but from my skin also. The flow of images that kept my brain humming all day long slowed down, then faded. A milky film replaced it, trying to find its way from my brain to my arteries, and little by little peace began dripping inside them.

I slept for a long, long time, emptied of all words and images. I remember only a dream: in my cupped hands, I was holding not water, but milk, from a curiously white, foamy river, and splashing my face with it. Then I took a mirror from my pocket and looked, but instead of my image, a face with no traits was staring at me, white and empty. It *was* a face and it was *mine*, but my features seemed to have disappeared into the whiteness of sleep, leaving behind a blurred, absence-filled image. *I* was that absence. Frozen with terror, I screamed, and the scream woke me up. My mother was next to me, trying to appease me, and when I asked what she was doing there, she laughed,

"What do you mean? I *live* here."

"And Alda?" I asked. "Where is Alda?"

"*You are Alda*," my mother replied.

False Memories of Not-Myself

> "To live is to be another ... To feel today the same thing as yesterday, it is to be today the living corpse of what was yesterday's life, already lost ..."
>
> Fernando Pessoa
> *The Book of Disquiet*

I *remember*: I must have been eight or nine. I remember opening the big cabinet where my parents kept their files and searching, convinced that I would eventually find the document of my adoption. I didn't find anything, and although I know that I am the child of my parents, part of me is still convinced—and no document in the world could convince me of the contrary—that I came from somewhere else and, through some mysterious law of chance, was entrusted to my parents, who thus became my legal guardians, the guardians of the cell that is my life.

All my life is but a series of innumerable episodes through which I tried, desperately tried, to escape this cell.

The country where I was born has no name. In this country, names don't exist. Language is but a fluid circulating between trees and people, people who aren't named, and trees that aren't "trees." The country of my birth doesn't exist. And then, *I*, I don't exist either, *I* is nothing but this knowledge that I drag behind me like the rotten tail of a crocodile changed into a parrot. The parrot is me. The parrot is a bird that repeats words it doesn't understand.

At school, they used to call me by *my name*. My last name. I was always petrified when I heard this name thrown at me like a rock at a wingless bird. I felt as if a thousand chains were tying me down to the country. Not-me to the not-my-country.

I never wanted anything *mine*. Not for lack of desire or greed—oh, no—but because "mine" seemed the very chain that tied one down to "my" land, "my" home, "my" children, the very chain of prescriptive existence that was nonexistence itself. As far as I was concerned, life had always been *on the other side*. The side which was not mine.

One of my first memories is that of our neighbor, a crazy man who used to walk with a camera around his neck and whom I so dreaded that the very thought of seeing him in the courtyard, when no one else was around, caused me panic and anxiety. One day, an aunt of mine told me he thought he was Jesus Christ, and from then on the image of a man walking around with a camera around his neck makes me think of a crazy man who takes himself for Jesus. His head, tilted to one side, was unusually long, cartoonish, and his dark eyes followed me like the eye of a hidden ever-present camera.

The presence of this eye that followed me during the first years of my childhood was accompanied at night by a sound reverberating in ebbs and flows throughout the house, a sound whose origin was a mystery, and which began like a murmur one could barely make out only to soon reach vibrations that shook the furniture and settled on it. Years later, I understood it was my grandfather's snoring.

***

I grew up surrounded by people who were, very likely, not much different from most people around the world. All men and women after a certain age had a swollen belly, a sign that, in spite of their normalness and apparent goodness, they occasionally ate children, who proved hard to digest and, as a consequence, remained imprisoned inside them like Jonah in the whale's stomach. They were nice people, especially the women, who were always eager to lend you a bit of sugar or flour, depending on the circumstances, or even money, who would take care of your progeny almost with a maternal tenderness while you were at work, and who, with the same undiminished ardor, would write anonymous letters to the neighborhood police to inform the authorities that you were a traitor and a spy. Not that they liked to write, no. In fact, for the most part they were illiterate. But they wanted to participate in the life of the community, and what ties a community together better than lying and denouncing?

Dictatorships have nothing to do with what we call "ideology;" the only ideology of those living under them is that of survival. Collaborators are made of the same stuff as those who, in democratic regimes, are only guilty of occasionally disgusting us with their appetite for success, which in their veins has taken the place of blood, with their conditioned-unconditional reflex of bowing down before Power, those who, under more austere skies, would be forced to put their appetite in the service of the butchers. Observe the servile grimace of your charming colleague whenever she is in the presence of one on whom her promotion depends, observe how zealously she drones on, her words sanctified by the seal of some fashionable authority, and try to imagine the same colleague in a country in which the only way of rising to the top is by stepping on the dead bodies of others. Those who "resist" under dictatorships are those whose only power is that of silencing their survival instinct, those for whom career and honors, that is, the recognition of one's ego, mean nothing or not enough, or those who are already at the edge of society and have nothing to lose. Each time I find myself before someone who displays great pride in the big leather armchair she is sitting in, I wonder what they would have done in other circumstances, another country, another time.

Then again, there are people, like my parents, who couldn't care less about the chair they are sitting on—as a matter of fact, they would prefer to be chairless if they saw someone in need of a chair—yet, they would always be on the side of Power for the simple reason that for some people—and they may be the majority—it somehow seems indecent to go against the grain.

My mother was half Hungarian and spoke Romanian with a heavy accent. On top of that, she always spoke as if we were all deaf, so, when we were in public, I pretended I didn't know this woman of shameless appearance with dyed red hair, who addressed everyone with a gregarious familiarity and revealed incidents that happened at home, laughing at her own jokes. We never knew what my father was, for he was, as my mother always said, a bastard. All we knew was that he wasn't a Gypsy. "We are not Gypsies," was the refrain my mother repeated, as if someone had stated the contrary.

One day, I opened the door and found myself before a babushka with a face furrowed by creases, head wrapped in a black kerchief, feet in dirty rubber galoshes. I called my mother, who, mouth open in surprise, invited her in. The woman entered, carrying a heavy bag and a small suitcase fastened with a piece of string and threatening to fall apart at any moment. She put the suitcase down and opened the bag, from where she took out a jar of pickles. This woman was my grandmother.

Since my parents worked, the task of taking care of the old woman fell to me. At first, I was a little scared of this Sphinx-like creature, all dressed in black, who exuded an odor of closed barn. But soon I understood that she had no power—a black mystery seated all day long on a chair—and that I, on the other hand, had unlimited power over her. Thus, I began to invent all kinds of little tortures, locking her up for hours in her room and not letting her use the bathroom, or keeping her without food. She never said anything to my mother, never complained. When she left, several months later, as she said good-bye, she touched my arm lightly and looked at me without a word, her eyes infinitely sad and heavy with tears. I can still see her eyes.

I grew up in the shadow of my twin sister, Hilda, who died at birth. I never managed to shake off the thought that maybe it was not she who died, but I, and the nurses made an understandable mistake. I sometimes wonder if my parents or anyone else suspects that I am the dead child, and that Hilda is among us, secretly alive.

All my dolls were called Helga—I couldn't bring myself to call them Hilda—but their name was known to no one but me. Little by little, the thought that maybe the death of my sister had been somehow caused by me, that I was the hidden cause of her death, began to take hold of me not only in daytime but also at night, in my dreams. A permanent anxiety was stuck in my chest, and I kept wondering whether I was the only one to know this, whether I was condemned to die with this secret. Did my mother know it, was this the hidden reason of her constant dissatisfaction with me, and if she knew, why did she keep quiet? And all the while, another thought as persuasive as the first: Hilda is alive and it's you who are dead.

It was pure coincidence that my first friend was called Gilda. But our bond was much more than the normal puerile friendship of two five-year-olds, for she was my very double. We even looked alike, or so people said, and spent hours together in such a perfect intimacy that sometimes minutes and hours melted away and no words were spoken. We knew time only when we were apart, and then we rushed toward each other to abolish it. But time stopped the day when all of a sudden and with no obvious explanation, Gilda's head got twisted and stuck to one side, as if someone had tried to pull it off by twisting it. I remember watching her, helpless and horrified, and trying to untwist her head, and then her yell of pain and the hurried steps of the adults. She stayed in the hospital for months and no one bothered to tell me how she was doing. My parents' answers were evasive, "They moved to another city," and I couldn't believe she would go away without telling me, and I cried for months and sacrificed all my dolls by burying them, hoping that the gods might be appeased. One day, someone casually mentioned "Gilda's bizarre death," and that was the last time I heard her name.

For a long time afterwards I had no friends. From the age of five to nine, my only friend was a hole in the wall to which I spoke at night before falling asleep.

At kindergarden there was an enormous gym whose floor hid a door opening onto a cave almost as big as the room itself, full of potatoes, and where one could spot every now and then two women peeling them. I knew that these women, whose light garments were in contrast with the cave's darkness, were witches, and I couldn't understand how no one seemed to care. One day, one of the instructors punished a boy by locking him up in the cave. It was only at night that someone remembered, "Say, where is ...?" and then, all the instructors hurried to the cave, from where they took out the boy's body, dead, his hair all gray.

I have a friend. She is a hole in the wall. A hole in the wall. And *you*, what are you? You are not even a hole in the wall. You are less than a hole. *Less than one*, oh yes, infinitely less.

My mother's friends often came to play bridge or Hungarian dominoes and chat about everything and nothing. Most of the time they gossiped about others with a perverse pleasure in which pure meanness was mixed with the amoral innocence of those poor in spirit. If the friends happened to be Russian, my mother would complain about the Germans, the Poles, the Moldavians, and the Jews, "who were destroying our country and selling it to the foreigners." If the friends happened to be German, she would complain about the Russians, the Poles, the Moldavians, and the Jews. If our Romanian relatives were over, she would curse the Hungarians, and vice-versa. Of course, sometimes she would get confused and curse the Hungarians when they were there, and then a wind of unease would blow for a second, but then, someone would remember the Gypsies, and they would all start cursing the Gypsies and the ethnic harmony would soon be reinstated.

Years later, when my mother came to see me in the States, it didn't take her long to recreate her Eastern European microcosm, and adapted—for Eastern European versatility should never be underestimated—her repertoire to the new landscape. Now, blacks were at the top of her list. The order of the people on the list changed according to circumstances and mood. Interestingly, the people who seemed to enjoy a special status for my mother and her friends were Native Americans. "Now, *these* are noble people," my mother would say, underlying "these" in a way that suggested that "other" people were far from sharing the same nobility. I sometimes wondered why she had such a fondness for Native Americans. Maybe because she didn't know any. Or maybe because most of these noble people were dead.

But sometimes, Mrs. Dubcheck or Mrs. Lensky would tell a tragic story in which the protagonist happened to belong to one of the blacklisted ethnicities, and then they would all reach for their handkerchiefs, and my mother would say, teary-eyed, "Well, we are all the same, aren't we? All God's creatures." And everybody would nod their heads in approval.

My mother was a hairdresser and my father—to the extent that he existed, which isn't certain—an accountant. When I met Laura, who reminded me of Gilda in an uncanny way, she asked me what my parents did for a living, and I answered without taking the time to think, "My parents are dead. They died in a car accident when I was two years old, and for several years I was raised by a circus troupe. We used to move from town to town. Now I live with an old aunt."

Laura's awe convinced me that I had struck at the right place, but it also caused me a great deal of anxiety. I was so afraid she might discover the truth and I would be humiliated that, although I loved her deeply, I began to secretly wish for her death. On the other hand, this secret we shared wrapped her in such a delicate aura that I almost told her an even bigger secret: that I, too, was dead and that her friend was not me but my sister Hilda.

One day the door swung open and, panting and puffing, my mother threw herself at me, hitting me, as she had done so many times, only this time infinitely angrier. She hit me, hissing through her teeth, "Dead, dead? You want your parents dead, is that it?" I understood that Laura had spoken and I was resigned to being punished. Being beaten was a lot less scary than being locked up in the red room like Jane Eyre. Since I had read this novel, which was the first one I ever read, I was Jane. Like her, I was an orphan, and my parents' existence was only a misunderstanding that would soon vanish.

Jane had a friend, Helen, who was kindness itself, and who, like all beings whose purity is not of this world, was tormented by the puritan, hypocrite teachers of the boarding school. She died of tuberculosis one night in Jane's arms, and ever since, my deepest desire was to elope and die together with my closest friend. On second thought ... Maybe my deepest desire was for my friend to die and for me to live to tell the story.

Laura and I went to the same school, a little school in the neighborhood, whose students, curious, frightening specimens of a lousy, destitute local population, had for us the mythical dimensions of half-beast half-human creatures against whom Laura and I struggled to defend ourselves during interminable school breaks. One day after classes we decided, in one of those moments of otherworldly elation that only the proximity of a close friend can bring, not to return home and to "run away." As we had no plan, we wandered aimlessly until sunset, when we were forced by our growling stomachs to find a solution. On the positive side, we were free to eat anything we wanted, only chocolate, if we so desired; on the negative side, we didn't have a penny. So, in order to better savor our newly found freedom, I forcefully stated that we *had* to eat chocolate, and proposed to beg in the street. Which we did, unsuccessfully, until a fat, ugly woman asked us what our names were and if our parents knew what we were doing.

As I said, my mother was Hungarian—or was she Bulgarian?—and didn't care much for all this "child sensitivity" talk of today. She used to say that "tears are from God" and according to an old custom, called the stick she beat me with "St. Nicholas." She would describe with a perverse pleasure how her father, whom she recalled with fondness, once whipped her back until blood sprang like a geyser. She was six and had stolen a flower.

If you are one of these people who use words like "abuse" or "let's talk about it" or "dysfunctional" or "X needs help," don't feel sorry for me; rather, feel sorry for yourself, for the language you are killing each time your mouth opens to repeat the already dying sounds masquerading as words in your elf-elp books, and for the blood that flows to your brain only to encounter the dead waters of mind's grotesque stillness. My childhood wasn't any worse than that of millions of other children; in fact, it was much better. My mother was a bitch, but at least she had a mind of her own.

We had a neighbor who was made of countless shadows that walked up and down the stairs like drunken ants. Her tracks were made of sorrow that spilled like black milk, and she talked to herself in a continuous dialogue in which a voice laughed hysterically, while the other quarreled angrily. Her children were dead. All three.

***

In my last visit to Transylvania I remember having seen a woman who was so old her back was curved in a perfect semicircle, and whose mouth whispered words in no known tongue. Her body was supported by a stick her hand held tightly, and her head was so close to the earth I was afraid she might accidentally touch it. She walked very slowly, her grayness barely visible on the gray sidewalk, and as I watched her, I realized she could never see the sky. All that she ever saw were people's shoes and the occasional thick spit on the ground.

"Travelers have no souls" (Yoko Tawada). Once, I was in a plane, returning from Europe, and I suddenly realized that my only possession, besides my body, was the luggage I had with me. I didn't have a key to any apartment, I hoped I could stay with a friend for a while, though I really didn't have any friends. Nor relatives. It was as if I had realized that I didn't exist—if one could say that. It wasn't a painful realization, on the contrary, it came as a lightness overcoming the darkness and heaviness of being. If the plane had exploded, we would have dissolved into thin air, and disappeared without a trace. I held my breath and tried to imagine being nothing but pure air, and I almost succeeded. Often, when I walk around and do things, I am nothing but pure-impure air. And something inside me keeps muttering, "not-a-soul-not-a-soul."

Before I left for the New World, a recurrent dream kept visiting me at night, again and again: a long, dark tunnel crossing the ocean, with a bizarre silhouette at its end. A man in black, his back turned to me, with a top hat on his head. He seemed strangely familiar, although I couldn't see his face. I knew in the dream that if I could guess who he was, the entire enigma of my future would be revealed. For years I kept thinking of that man, of who he was, and of how that might affect me. Then one day I saw a photo. The photo of the man in the dream. On its back one could read: "Fernando Pessoa (1888-1935)."

***

I once knew a man with whom I had the following dialogue:
"Who are you?"
"They call me 'the changing man.'"
"Why do they call you that?"
"Because I turn into whoever happens to be around me, like a chameleon."
"But why?"
"Maybe because I am no one."
"So who are you now?"
"According to some people, I am a Chinese man who looks like a white man, according to others, a Jew from Manhattan; my psychiatrist says it is because of my parents who used to lock me up in a closet."
"Does this mean I am a Chinese man or a Jew from Manhattan?"
"No, I think it means you should get a psychiatrist too."

I often look at office clerks, store employees and waiters, people I see for two or three minutes, then maybe never again, thinking that the person in front of me, *on the other side*, could have been me. That it was only an accident of chance or biology that I am not them, and I try to imagine being in their skin and in their brain, and *from their side* to look at myself as at a complete stranger. But no matter how hard I try to be the other person, always, always, a gap impossible to fill remains.

Ever since I was a child I was horrified by the *continuity* of existence, by existence incarnated in one unbearable form. It seemed to me that only by shedding skin after skin could one continue to really live, so I imagined existence as a *possibility*, and invented many lives for myself, and felt that I had to leave in order to live them. I yearned to leave. And I knew that once I arrived in a new place, I had to start killing it all over again. Killing space to renew time.

***

Naming is beginning. To erase and start all over again. "Portuguese language is my nation," he had said toward the end of his life. But what if one had *no nation*? No nation even in the marrow of one's bones, no language of one's own. Little by little, I began to fantasize that I could move from one language to another as if from one space to another. That I could recreate my very depths, the depths where naming begins. That when I said "I" no one spoke but the temporary *nation of shadow*, a language not my own. That my own was only the flitting instant covering the distance between two languages not my own.

On the twisted road between birth and death, consciousness is a tied-up animal, struggling and yelling at the indifferent passersby, "I exist! I! I!" And the passersby keep on, forever enclosed within the mocking silence of their impervious bodies. But *I*, I wrote this only to record the passage of my shadow on earth, for I have never existed.

What Would You Do?

Four friends gathered one day away from the world's madness—war in the Middle East, terrorist attacks everywhere, famine in Africa—in an apartment situated somewhere between the thirtieth and the fortieth floors of a skyscraper and, like the ten cheerful Italians who had congregated to escape plague six hundred and fifty years ago in the city of Florence, decided to pass the time by telling stories. But the stories of our friends had a theme and a provocation; they had to imagine an extraordinary situation as a background for a question addressed to all of them, "What would you do?"

This is the story told by the first of them:
What would you do if one day, upon returning home, you should find your pet monkey with your high-heels on, lips smeared with lipstick, and a cell phone in her hand, and when you tried to rescue the valuable instrument from her primitive hands she wouldn't let go, and instead, would begin to produce high-pitched warlike cries, and you would fight until, almost vanquished by her

animal strength, you would call for help and someone from your entourage would come, grab the phone and neutralize the noise-making hairy beast with a big slap on her head, but this would be only the beginning of an unbelievable emancipation of this otherwise cute little creature, and next time you would come home to find her dancing to the music coming from the headphones she had place d with methodical care on her big round ears, which appear even bigger and pinker than they normally are, and you would yell at her to take the God damn headphones off, but she is having too much fun, dancing and beating the air with her arms like a swimmer trying not to drown, and then you would put your hand on the headphones and pull, but the monkey would be even faster and catch your hand with skillful precision—she is a monkey after all—then twist it until you began to scream and someone else would come and twist the monkey's arm until she let go of both your arm and the headphones, and then you (that is, you and the monkey) look at each other like Cain at Abel before the murder and without quite knowing who is Cain and who is Abel, and you part knowing that it's not over yet and, indeed, one day you would find her seated in front of your computer, touching the keys with one hand and scratching her head with the other as she stares at the screen, and then you would finally understand, and go to the bathroom to look in the mirror, and you would see staring at you the image of a monkey, and you would stare back at her, and she at you, both forever imitating each other with the mirror standing between you as a transparent screen into which everything flows and everything turns into its twin and No One exists.

    This is the story told by the second:
    What would you do if one day, walking down the street, you should stop in front of a store window to admire a pair of imported leather shoes and, as you look at them, you suddenly see your reflection in the window and begin to make faces the way you sometimes do out of boredom before the bathroom mirror, and then stop and look again at the beautiful shoes, and when you are about to move away from the window you realize that your

previous grimace is still there, stuck on the window among the shoes, and you tell yourself that it must be an optical illusion and move several steps back, but the grimace is still there, and you let out a cry of surprise which triggers the attention of a passerby who stops and looks at you, then at the grimace, then at you, ever more puzzled, and he too lets out a cry of surprise and then another passerby stops and within minutes a whole crowd has gathered around you producing a noise that fills the street with a hair-rising chirping, the chirping of a drunken multiheaded mythical bird, and you try to explain that it's not your fault, that you were just admiring the shoes when your grimace got stuck on the window, and you tried to leave but the grimace wouldn't, and everyone is looking at you in disbelief shaking their heads and mumbling If it's not your fault why do you look so guilty, why, indeed, and the crowd becomes more and more menacing, and then a cop arrives out of nowhere, and orders everyone to move aside, and advances toward you with measured orderly steps, and you begin to tell the whole story from the beginning, how you were walking down the street, etc., and the more you talk the more inquisitive the cop's eyes become, staring at you like the eyes of a dead fish, and in the summer heat the fishy odor rises in the air and the crowd slowly withers away, and the cop barks That's enough, follow me, and you feel your legs softening under you and your heartbeat stops for an instant then resumes with maddened speed and you open your mouth to say that it's not your fault, but your eyes meet the cop's fish eyes and your mouth clenches and, shaking with terror, you follow him and leave behind the stubborn grimace as you slowly disappear into the crowd.

This is the story told by the third:
What would you do if one summer day, sitting on the terrace of your favorite café and watching with professional interest—you are a writer—the other customers while you wait for the arrival of your friend, you should notice at the table next to you one of those blond families that fill the city's downtown streets in the summer, with two teenage girls blabbering joyously about ... it's impossible

to say what because you only hear bits and pieces and anyhow it doesn't matter these people seem to have been mass produced by the same factory, and you are about to mumble Americans, but you remember that now you are an American too and your blond wife even looks a little bit like them, so you swallow your remark and rest your eyes on the middle-aged woman with dark hair and glasses occupying the table at your left, impossible to say from what country, she could be from anywhere, Italy, France, America, South America, Eastern Europe, the Middle East, and you wonder what is it about intelligence that makes it so devoid of ethnic or national characteristics, while stupidity seems so *rooted* in one place, but before you have the chance to come up with an answer your friend arrives with a newspaper under his arm and tells you about the last dead and that the total number is now three hundred, and you both start discussing with animation and after you have exhausted the topic you move to celebrity gossip and then to the gossip of smaller and smaller circles until you are down to yourselves, but by then your lives seem so trivial that you don't even want to bother and go back to international politics and you both make the comment at the same time The world is such a mess and how lucky we are to live here, but at the very instant when you say these words everything turns to leaden gray, no it's not possible, and yet it is, suddenly that omniscient voice present in our dreams, which is half yourself half another or maybe no one, says But this is happening here, here … and suddenly you are walking through debris and your friend doesn't stop talking and you realize that it's all happening here here and you wake up drenched in sweat God what a nightmare, you need an hour to readjust to the quiet normality of your surroundings, and after you drink your coffee and finally feel better you go to the local newsstand to buy the daily paper, and on your way home you open it and see that your country is at war and over three hundred people are dead and several cities have been destroyed, and you tell yourself that you must still be dreaming and touch yourself to see if you can feel anything, and what you feel is pain everywhere, could you be wounded, you ask yourself, looking to see if there is blood on you, no blood, thank God, you whisper but the pain doesn't go away, it weighs on your chest pressing it into the ground until, terrorized that you will end up buried under it, you wake up drenched in sweat, God what a nightmare, when will this end, and go to the kitchen where everything is normal no debris no corpses, it was only a dream, and you drink your cup of coffee and turn on the TV where corpses swim in a blue sea of electrons—although you're not quite sure what an electron is, but you think it must have something to do with electricity and these are electric corpses, and the war vibrates with electric sophistication on the ocean-blue screen, and you wonder how long it will be until it spills over the frame, for you know it's only a question of time.

This is the story told by the fourth:
What would you do if one day you should be talked into meeting three other friends in a high-rise office building that usually swarms with people except on that day because it's a holiday and no one is there, not even the security guard, and you take the elevator up to the thirty-something floor, and walk down the empty hall with glossy cream linoleum and bare walls, then enter the office where your friends have been waiting for you including the one who had the idea of coming there on such a day, and you chat for a while then try to get more details about the rules of the game, but the friend says that all you have to do is tell a story and there is nothing to worry about, and all of a sudden you start to worry, wondering why did he say worry, and you look at his face noticing for the first time the unfocused gaze which moves from point to point without settling on anything, the pink tip of his nose exuding an obscenity similar to a monkey's behind, and you feel your inner organs move aside to make space for a big emptiness inside you a dizzying hollow gap, and it is as if you are falling into this hole pulled into a vortex of nothingness while your friends are chatting and laughing merrily, and the fourth friend says Let me show you something, and he takes you all to the door explaining that it locks automatically and there is no way out from the inside, and then he shows you the enormous glass windows

covering an entire wall, improperly called "windows" because they are designed not to open, and he tells you again there is no way out, and then you and the other two friends exchange glances, and one of them asks What do you mean there is no way out, and the fourth friend laughs and says I knew you were going to say that; simply: no way out, and then the other friend clears his dry throat and asks the fourth one Why did you do this, and the fourth one answers You always said I have no sense of humor. Well, you were wrong.

From the Diary of an Accidental Housewife

Notes on How to Boil an Egg

First, take an egg. Small, medium or large, white or brown. Happy or unhappy chicken—it doesn't matter. The important thing is for the egg not to be cracked. Turn the egg on all its … all its … on all its (let's call them "sides" so we can move on) and make sure it's a healthy, smooth, crack-free egg. You may be tempted to rush this phase, but you would be making a grave mistake, for the success of the entire proceeding depends on it. As I said, make sure there are no eggs in the crack. I mean, no cracks in the egg. Then move on to the second phase.

Take a medium-size pot … take a medium … or maybe a small, a small would do it, so, take a medium or a small-size pot, fill it with water up to … up to a certain point, then … wait … Was it hot or cold water? Hot or cold water? I really don't remember. I don't. Let's say it was cold, because from cold water you can make hot water, but not the other way around. Wait … actually, you can.

As I was saying, put some hot or cold water into the pot, then put the egg ... No. Don't put the egg anywhere. No. How could you *not* put the egg anywhere? It has to be *somewhere*. Put the egg somewhere, but not in the pot. But remember where you put it because if you don't you won't be able to find it afterwards to put it in the pot, and without an egg you can't make a boiled egg. You could make a boiled egg without a pot, but not without an egg. You could even make a boiled egg without water—you could boil it in milk, for instance—but, once again, not without an egg. Therefore make sure you remember what basket you put your egg in so you know where to find it to boil it.

While your egg comfortably rests somewhere—but not in the pot—put the pot on the stove, turn on the gas—make sure you turn on the burner under the pot and not one of the others, as happens so often—and wait for the water to boil. In order for the water to boil the flame needs to be on high, and you have to wait two or three minutes. There is a very easy way of recognizing if the water is boiling: you will notice some small bubbles, first at the edge of the pot, then gradually moving toward the center, then everywhere.

There they are: the bubbles. They make a little fizzy sound resembling nothing else but boiling water. What are they made of, you wonder. Well, water of course. What else? You wonder what the bubble itself is made of. Air? Air surrounded by water. That's why it's called a bub-ble. It's like trying to speak underwater.

Now that the water is boiling, it's time to put the egg in the pot. Take the egg from where you had placed it ... take the egg... If you can find it, take the egg and put it in the pot. Where is that damn egg? It's always the same. After all this effort, after checking the egg all over for cracks, after putting the water into the pot and the pot on the stove and the egg aside, after boiling the water, right at the end when you're almost there, the egg has disappeared. It happens again and again. You look all over the counter, on the table, in the cabinets, even in the dishwasher. The egg is gone. How is it possible for an egg to disappear just like that? To completely vanish from the face of the earth? You could, of course, take another egg, but you cannot give up like that. Accept defeat without fighting. And then, you would have to start all over again: check the egg for cracks, put some more water into the pot because it has almost entirely evaporated, wait for the water to boil and then ... Then hope that the egg is still there. Somewhere.

Notes on How to Throw a Dinner Party

Start by inviting several guests. No more than four and no fewer than two. If you invite more than four you'll have to deal with a large pile of dishes later, unless the guests insist on washing the dishes themselves, and in my experience this is even worse because they always mix things up, use the wrong sponge or dishcloth or put them in the wrong place, and my husband cannot stand things that aren't in their proper place. Once, we had a guest who kept insisting on washing the dishes, a very nice man in his sixties. He was used to washing them at home, you see, his wife is French and tells him what to do and he does it, so he kept saying, "I'll do the dishes," until my husband exploded, "I don't want you to wash any fucking dishes." Our friend was so traumatized he stopped washing dishes altogether, his wife washes them now.

So, as I was saying, no more than four, but no fewer than two guests. You'll understand why no fewer than two when you hear this story. Once, many years ago, I invited two friends, a couple, for dinner. When they arrived I realized there was no bread, so I excused myself and ran to the bakery at the street corner—this was in Europe, you could just run downstairs and in five minutes be back with a loaf of bread. But after I bought the bread, as I was walking back home, something happened. Suddenly I realized I couldn't do it and I couldn't explain why. I pictured myself opening the door and engaging in small talk with them, then cutting the bread and placing it on the table, bringing the food and then ... what? I just couldn't play the film forward, I stood there in the middle of the room, paralyzed, with a pot in my hands, and the guests staring at me and waiting for me to do something. And I didn't know what to do. Suddenly, these friends whom I'd known for years morphed into giant creatures with huge heads from which several pairs of eyes were staring at me, they weren't friends any longer, they were GUESTS. And I could see myself look at them and them at me, waiting for me to do something. I was *expected to do something*. But what?

I have no problem with being a guest, I can do that very well. I eat everything you put on my plate, and sometimes I even ask for more, unless there is very little left, and then I politely decline any invitation to help myself. If the hostess says, "Let's go in the other room," I go in the other room. If the hostess offers wine, I drink wine and don't ask for beer. I have no special culinary requests. I eat anything. Sometimes—but very rarely—I even offer to wash the dishes; but I don't insist and I usually say it in a low voice, hoping that no one will hear.

So, you see, I am a very good guest. But when you are the host, the roles are reversed, and the guest is expecting you to tell her what to do. This is the root of my problem, I think. I have no desire to tell people what to do, what to eat, no desire to offer them anything. Not as much because I am lazy—though I can't honestly entirely eliminate this hypothesis—but for reasons ... how should I put it? Ontological reasons. I can't say, "Would you like some more?" I've tried, but it always comes out the wrong way, because I mumble and no one hears it, or else I shout, and the guests are scared to say no, so everyone says yes, and then there isn't enough food to go around.

I am always puzzled by women who seem so at ease in their kitchen, talking with their guests while attending to some dish on the stove, as if it were the most natural thing to do, smiling, laughing, taking a sip of wine, making sure everyone gets the drink of their choice—wine, beer, orange juice, cranberry juice, tomato juice, mineral water—how can you do that without getting mixed up? I never give people a choice, otherwise I would get so confused we would end up spending the whole night trying to figure out who gets what.

So I pictured myself in the middle of the room with my mouth open, struggling to say, "Would you like some more?" but the words wouldn't come out—how can one say "Would you like some more?" and what is the appropriate tone of voice when saying it? It was like that day when something happened in my French class—I was a French teacher, you know. Something very similar. I raised my hand holding a pen, and I opened my mouth to say, "*C'est un stylo*," and all of a sudden I froze with my hand in the air and I couldn't say anything. I just looked at my hand, petrified by the absurdity of it all. How can one say, "This is a pen" in front of thirty pairs of eyes staring at you? How much more ridiculous than that can one get? So, I stood there holding the pen without a word for what seemed like an eternity, and everyone was staring, and you couldn't hear a pen drop.

So, you see, this is why that day I couldn't go back with the loaf of bread and face the guests who were waiting for me. Instead, I hid in a dark nook in a coffee shop and stayed there for several hours, thinking that at some point the guests must realize I wasn't going to come back, and they'd leave. Luckily there were two of them, so they could keep each other company. Imagine if there had been only one. The guest waiting for the host to come, waiting and waiting, and the host never shows up. That's why, as I was saying, never invite fewer than two guests.

Notes on Ironing

Take an ironing board and a Sunbeam Steam Master iron. Open the board's legs, place it in a steady position by the wall, and put the iron on top of it. Take a cup of water and pour it into an orifice preferably identified beforehand in the front part of the iron, trying not to spill too much water around. Plug the iron into the electric outlet, then switch the round knob to the desired temperature. While the iron is getting hot, place the shirt on the ironing board, smoothing its surface with your fingers. Touch delicately the iron's base to see if it's hot enough; remove your finger promptly.

After this preliminary phase, take the iron in your right hand, pressing on the shirt with your left, and move the iron in circles on the shirt's surface. You will notice with considerable pleasure that the shirt is getting softer and its wrinkles are disappearing. Then, you will remark that in the process of smoothing out a small surface, you have inadvertently produced some wrinkles at the edges of the ironed area. You will, of course, attempt to eliminate said wrinkles, and after some effort you will succeed, but then you'll detect that in doing so, another set of small wrinkles has appeared in another corner. By then you will have understood that a wrinkle-free shirt is impossible to obtain through a normal ironing procedure, and that you have to accept a compromise. So you try to ignore the minor wrinkles, concentrating instead on the big ones. You turn the shirt on the other side only to notice with increased aggravation that it has more wrinkles than it had at the beginning, and you repeat everything you had done with the other side. After several minutes the shirt looks much better, smoother and shinier, but you are afraid to turn it over and examine all the wrinkles you have likely created in the process. Very carefully you lift a corner and take a peek. You see a big wrinkle running diagonally across the entire shirt, but the rest looks almost acceptable. You put the iron down next to the shirt. You go to the office and take a fifteen-pound Spanish-English/English-Spanish Oxford Dictionary, return to the ironing board and lay down the dictionary on the shirt. You breathe with relief, wondering why you hadn't thought of this from the beginning.

Word of advice: *under no circumstances* should you put the iron on the dictionary! Remember to take the dictionary back to the shelf before your husband comes home! Remember to unplug the iron!

Notes on How to Give Birth (or Not)

Of course, for this one you first need to get pregnant. When your time comes—and, under normal circumstances it should come no longer than nine months after conception, although my mother claims I was born almost at ten months, I simply didn't want to come out, and after I did, I understood why—check yourself into a maternity ward and do what they tell you. I won't go into details here: if you ever get pregnant, you'll see for yourself; if not, you don't need to know them.

So, let's skip the details and zoom in to the scene where I am doing what every woman who wants to rid herself of that huge belly does: push. I see faces around me, grotesquely deformed, as if by Luna Park mirrors or as if they were figures in a Francis Bacon painting, and they all say, "Push, push."

And then, suddenly, all desire to push leaves me. I simply don't feel like pushing anymore.

"What happened?" asks the doctor.

"I don't want to push anymore."

He stares, incredulous.

"Why?" he asks, after several seconds of puzzled silence.

As my answer doesn't come, I see my husband move closer to him and whisper in his ear, "She's very stubborn. We should …" I don't hear the rest, but then my husband turns toward me with an uncharacteristically soft voice: "OK. Don't push anymore, if you don't want to." As if I didn't know his tricks! He thinks that now I'm going to push just to spite him. So, I say smiling, "OK. I'm not pushing."

Then the three of us, my husband, the doctor and myself stay there, staring at each other, me not pushing, and them exchanging furtive glances, interrupted occasionally by: "So, you still don't want to push?"

"No, I don't."

"OK then."

Then the doctor lights a cigarette and my husband pulls out a pack of cards from his vest pocket, and they start playing poker. I watch them for a while; then, as I begin to get bored, I ask if I can join in. The doctor furrows his brow looking interrogatively at my husband, and mumbles something like, "I don't think that in your condition it's a very good idea. But if your husband agrees …"

"Oh, she does as she pleases," he says. "As she pleases," he repeats.

We played until night settled in and forced us to turn on the lights. The doctor looked at his watch and jumped up rushing to the door, then disappeared in the dark hall advising me to "take it easy." For once, I followed a doctor's advice. The next day I checked out of the hospital without ever pushing again. The baby has been with me ever since, and as far as I can tell has no intention of coming out into the world. And why would she (it is a "she," of course)? What better place to be than in a mother's womb, a seed of nothingness in store for future being?